CARAM3-AT_0900-45TGFEK-5-THKK-90
3K-HJB4T556-0-5PD045899-LG0-A0LZ
TEBS-32-89-JKLDD_09021-JK05-4-465

MARVEL
CAPTAIN AMERICA
THE WINTER SOLDIER

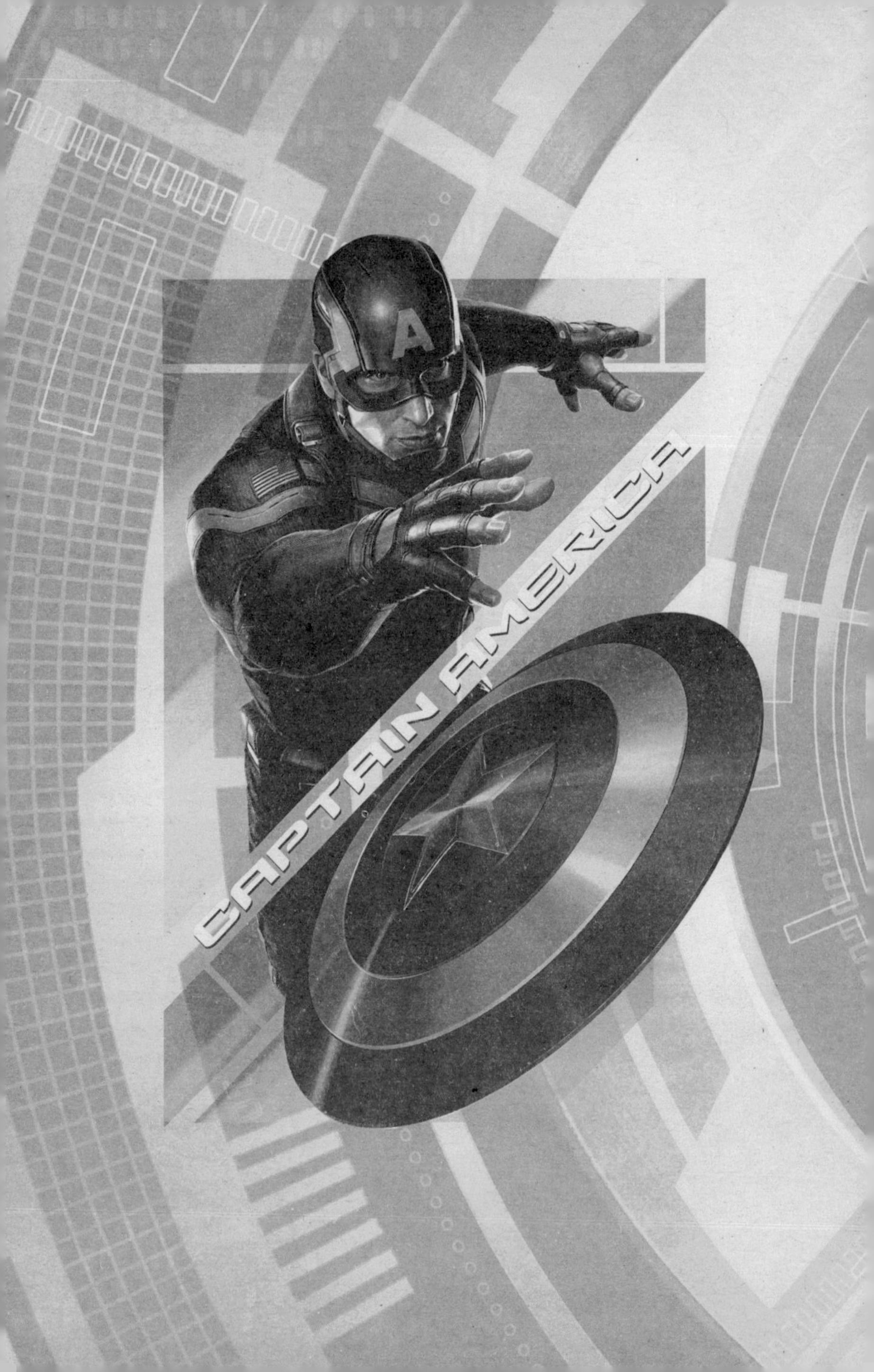
CAPTAIN AMERICA

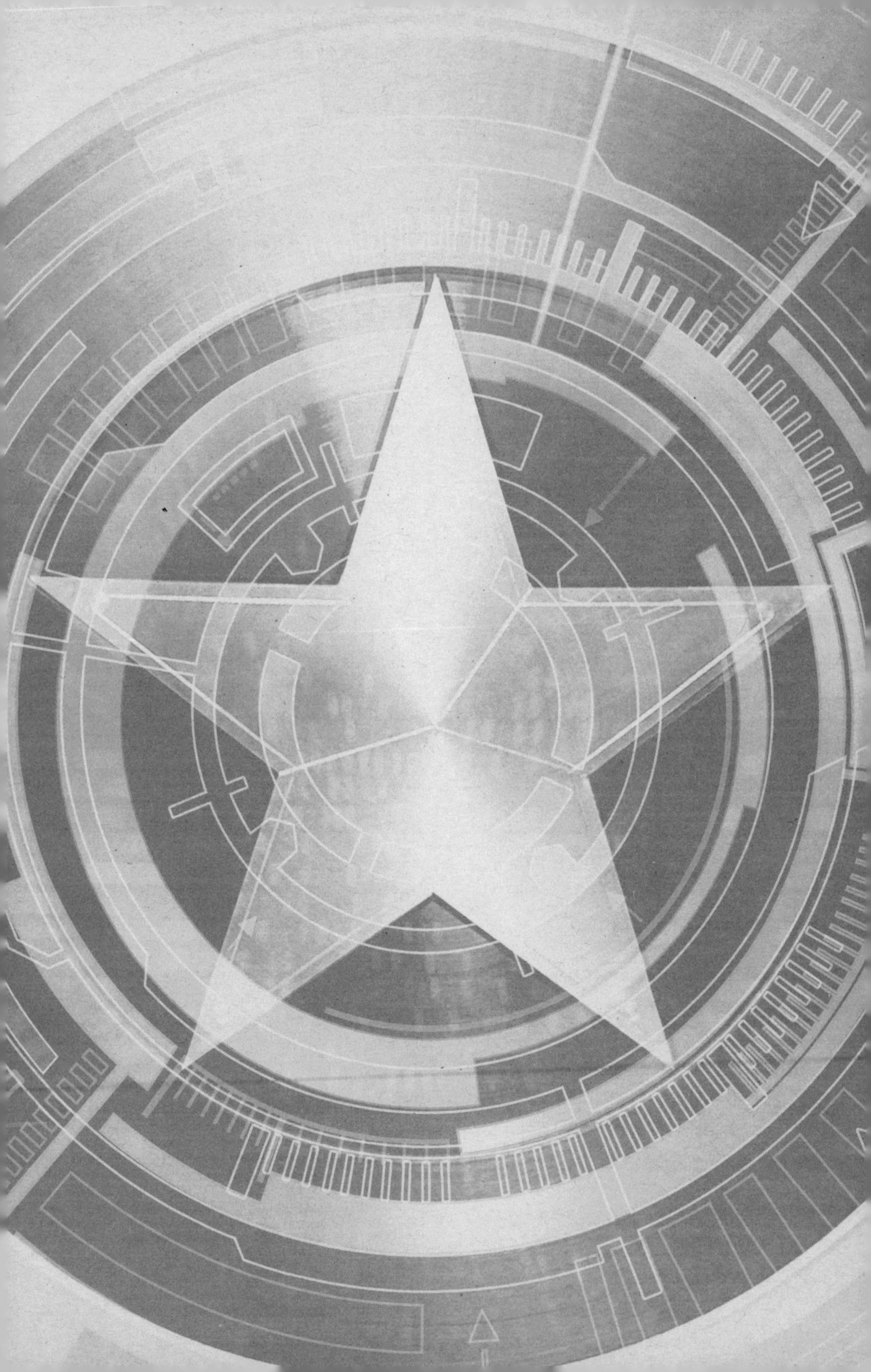

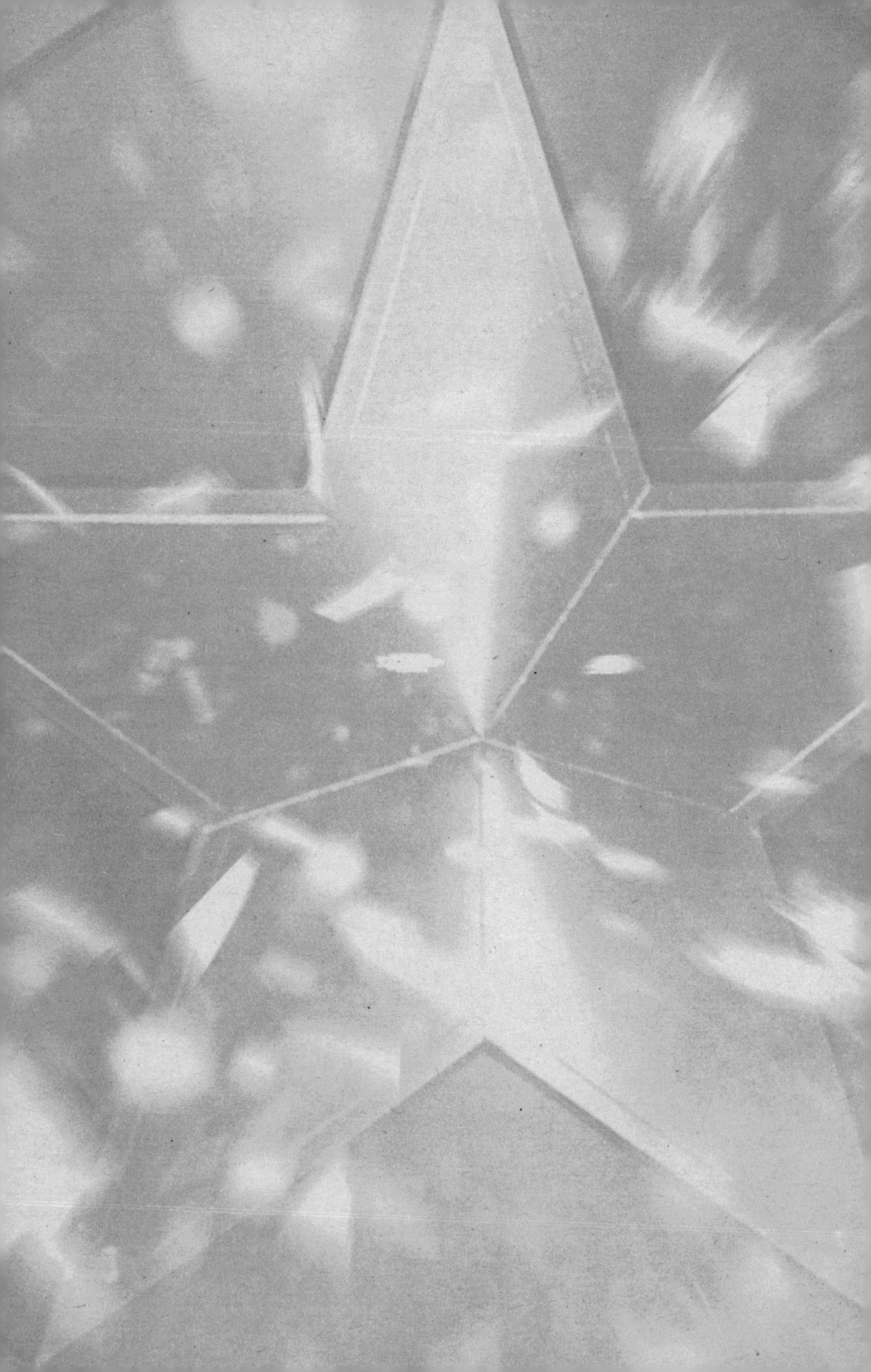

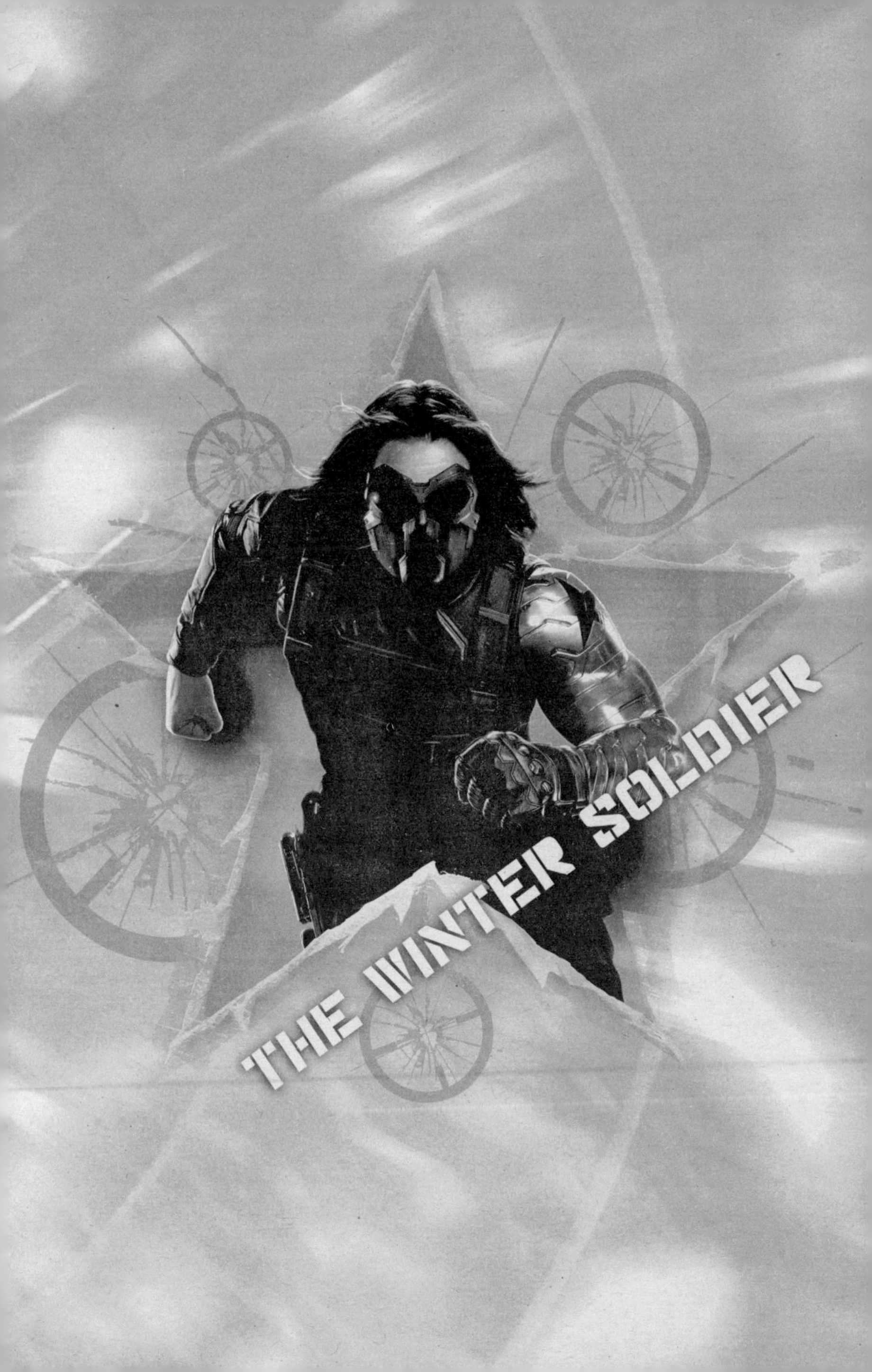
THE WINTER SOLDIER

2-00-5_UUIGGE_67-8990

MARVEL
CAPTAIN AMERICA
THE WINTER SOLDIER

ADAPTED BY
Allison Lowenstein and Tomas Palacios

BASED ON THE SCREENPLAY BY
Christopher Markus & Stephen McFeely

PRODUCED BY
Kevin Feige, p.g.a.

DIRECTED BY
Anthony and Joe Russo

MARVEL

NEW YORK · LOS ANGELES

MARVEL

© 2014 MARVEL

Printed in the United States of America

First Edition

1 3 5 7 9 10 8 6 4 2

V475-2873-0-14015

ISBN 978-1-4231-8533-8

SUSTAINABLE
FORESTRY
INITIATIVE

Certified Chain of Custody
Promoting Sustainable Forestry

www.sfiprogram.org
SFI-01054
The SFI label applies to the text stock

PARAM3-4T_8900-45IGFFK-3-TAKK-90
3K_HJ041556-0-5POO43099-LG0-A8LZ
TEBS-32-89-JKLDD_89021-JK85-4-465

MARVEL

CAPTAIN AMERICA
THE WINTER SOLDIER

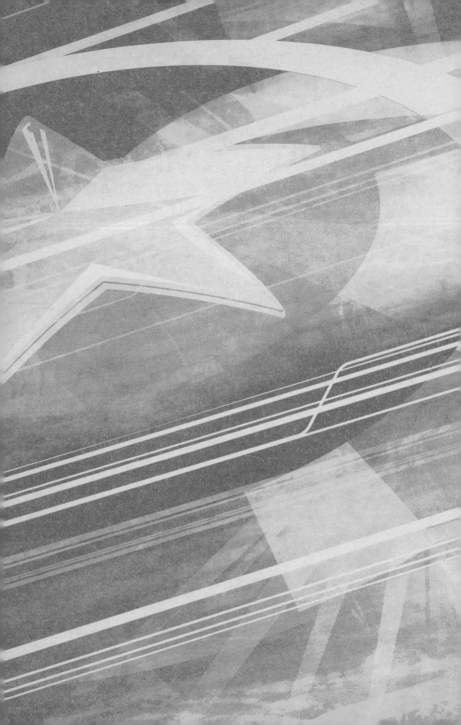

2-80-5_0UIGGE_67-8900

MEMORANDUM

To: S.H.I.E.L.D. Agent ████████████
From: Agent Sitwell
Subject: The Winter Soldier

During our investigation we recovered the following top secret files. These records have been obtained through S.H.I.E.L.D.'s most advanced form of spy technology: nano-camera and sound recorders, security cameras hacked by S.H.I.E.L.D. personnel, as well as recorders hidden in plain sight, in objects like pens, watches, phones, and computers, to name a few. After careful consideration, we have agreed to allow you limited access to these documents. This information is vital to the safety of S.H.I.E.L.D. As we look back at the events involving Operation: Winter Soldier, we can see the strengths and weaknesses of S.H.I.E.L.D., and in order for you to be a vital part of our organization, you must be able to analyze these files, both physical and digital, and understand their importance to the future of S.H.I.E.L.D. and the world.

Sincerely,

Agent Sitwell

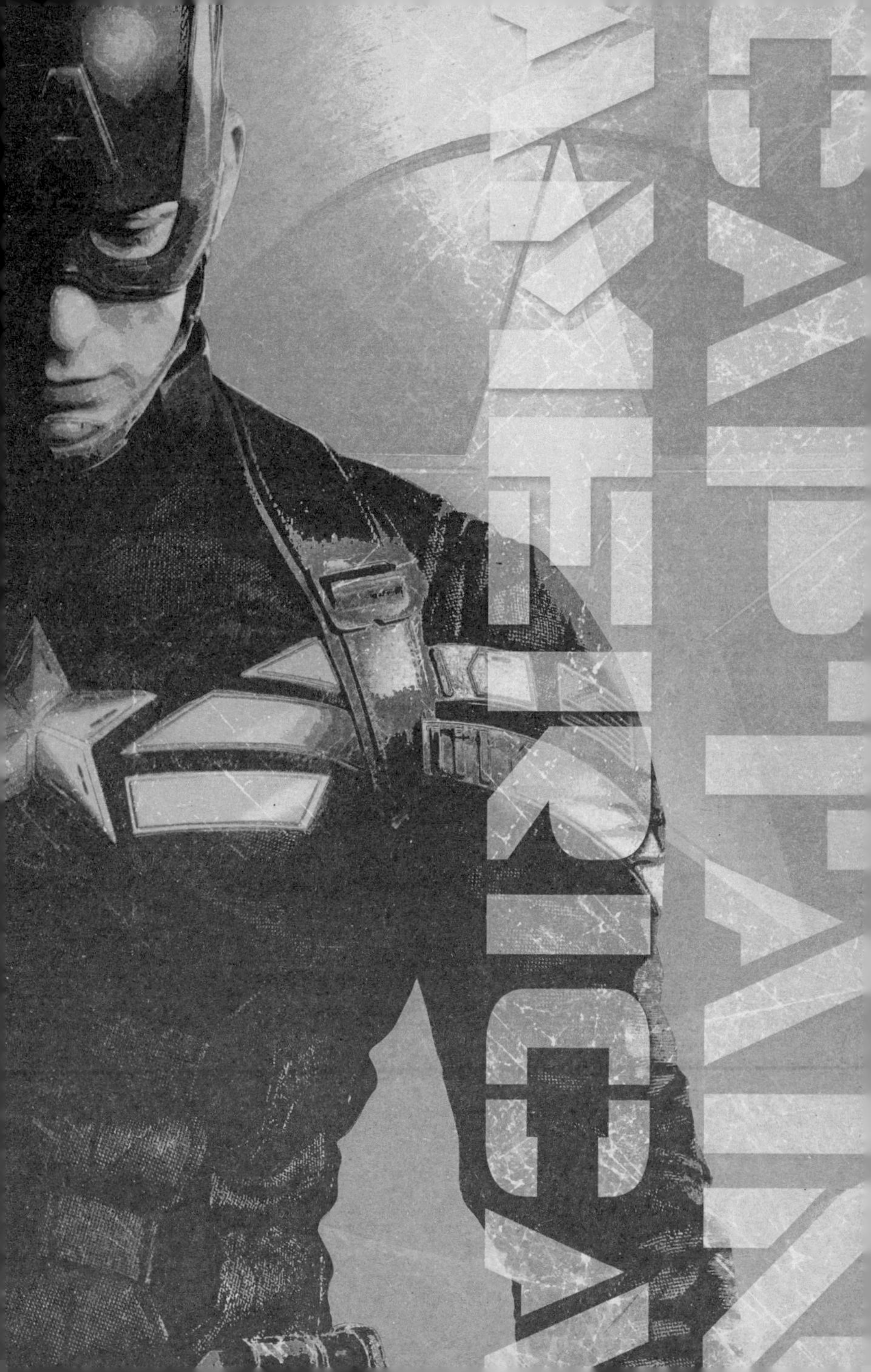
CAPTAIN
AMERICA

THE FIRST AVENGER

"Wars are fought with weapons but are won by men."
—General Patton

THE WORLD WAS AT WAR, and America was sending all its young men off to fight. Everywhere you went, you could see posters of Uncle Sam asking Americans to take their parts in the battle.

Steve Rogers, a scrawny and sickly kid from Brooklyn, just wanted to be a soldier. But his poor physical health prevented him from enlisting. He knew there were severe consequences for forging information during the draft process, yet that didn't stop him from traveling to various recruiting centers and trying to enlist. One recruiter after another grabbed a huge stamp and slammed it down on his form. The stamps all read the same: 4F—REJECTED. Knowing he could not apply twice at the same location, Steve said he was from Hoboken, New Jersey; Paramus, New Jersey; Brooklyn, New York: anywhere to try to get into the army. But the response was always the same: *You're not good enough. Not strong enough. Not fast enough. Not enough . . .*

Steve's best friend, James Buchanan, or, as his friends called him, Bucky, took Steve with him to the World Expo in hopes of cheering him up, but Steve left Bucky and wandered around on his own. Ironically, he found a recruiting center. There he met a genius scientist named Dr. Erskine, who told Steve he could get him into the army, but it would involve being a part of a very special project. After having attempted to enlist in five different cities, Steve accepted his offer. What did he have to lose? Steve asked the doctor why he chose such a small and scrawny person. His reply: "Because the strong man who has known power all his life may lose respect for that power, but a weak man knows the value of strength and knows . . . compassion."

At the same time, he met Peggy Carter, an agent of the Special Scientific Reserve who, like Steve, worked very hard to gain the respect she deserved in the army. She might not have been weak, but she was a woman. Women were supposed to stay home, but Peggy Carter was like Steve and wanted to help. Steve was smitten.

He felt like his life had just begun.

A few weeks into basic training, Dr. Erskine told Steve that he had created a Super-Soldier Serum, a serum that would grant him peak physical abilities. He informed Steve that the serum would not only affect his muscles; it would affect his cells as well and create a protective system of regeneration and healing. Steve's metabolism would burn four times faster than the average human's. The serum would amplify everything in the mind as well. So good would become great, but also, bad would become worse.

Steve had the mind and fortitude of a soldier, so,

fearless, he went into the lab and emerged a Super-Soldier. He was no longer a skinny kid; he was a muscular man who had the strength of an entire army! Dr. Erskine reminded Steve that he must stay who he was. Not a perfect soldier . . . but a good man.

Suddenly, a spy seated in the gallery of spectators observing the operation shot Dr. Erskine. Steve ran after the man and tracked him down. The spy was a part of HYDRA: a sinister organization bent on taking over the world. HYDRA was led by the Red Skull. Before Dr. Erskine came to America, he'd lived in Germany where he had created the Super-Soldier Serum and injected it into a German soldier during one of Erskine's early trials. The serum turned the man into the Red Skull, with a creepy red face and a heart that was driven by pure evil. It seemed the spy shot Erskine so he would not share the serum with anyone else. Red Skull wanted to be the only one with that power!

Steve Rogers wanted to go to Europe to fight HYDRA, but history repeated itself. Steve was told he couldn't fight. Instead, America used Steve as a spokesperson for the army. He became Captain America, a living Super Hero. There were comic books based on Captain America and a hugely popular traveling show in which Cap (as he was now called by the locals) showed his strength and his belief in the army. Captain America had become a song-and-dance act.

Finally, the Super-Soldier was sent to Europe, but it wasn't to fight in the war against HYDRA. Instead, it was to perform. Steve was upset and hurt when the real soldiers heckled him during his Captain America show. When Steve found out that all the soldiers were distressed because half their platoon had been captured, he empathized with them. Then he found out that his best friend, Bucky, was one of the abducted soldiers, and Steve decided to give up the life of a showman and start the life of a soldier!

Armed with a shield created by inventor Howard Stark (the father of Tony Stark, aka Iron Man), Cap went deep into battle, fighting HYDRA and Red Skull and saving the platoon. Sadly, Bucky perished while fighting the enemy. He and Steve had an intense battle against HYDRA aboard a speeding train somewhere in Europe. On a later mission, Steve Rogers crashed a plane that doubled as a hydrogen bomb somewhere in Antarctica. The First Avenger, Captain America, sacrificed his own life to save his country and the world.

Seventy years later, Nick Fury and S.H.I.E.L.D. went to Antarctica after discovering a weird anomaly in the ice. They dug it up and discovered Captain America. Now, awake and adjusting to the twenty-first century, this Super-Soldier is ready to fight for freedom.

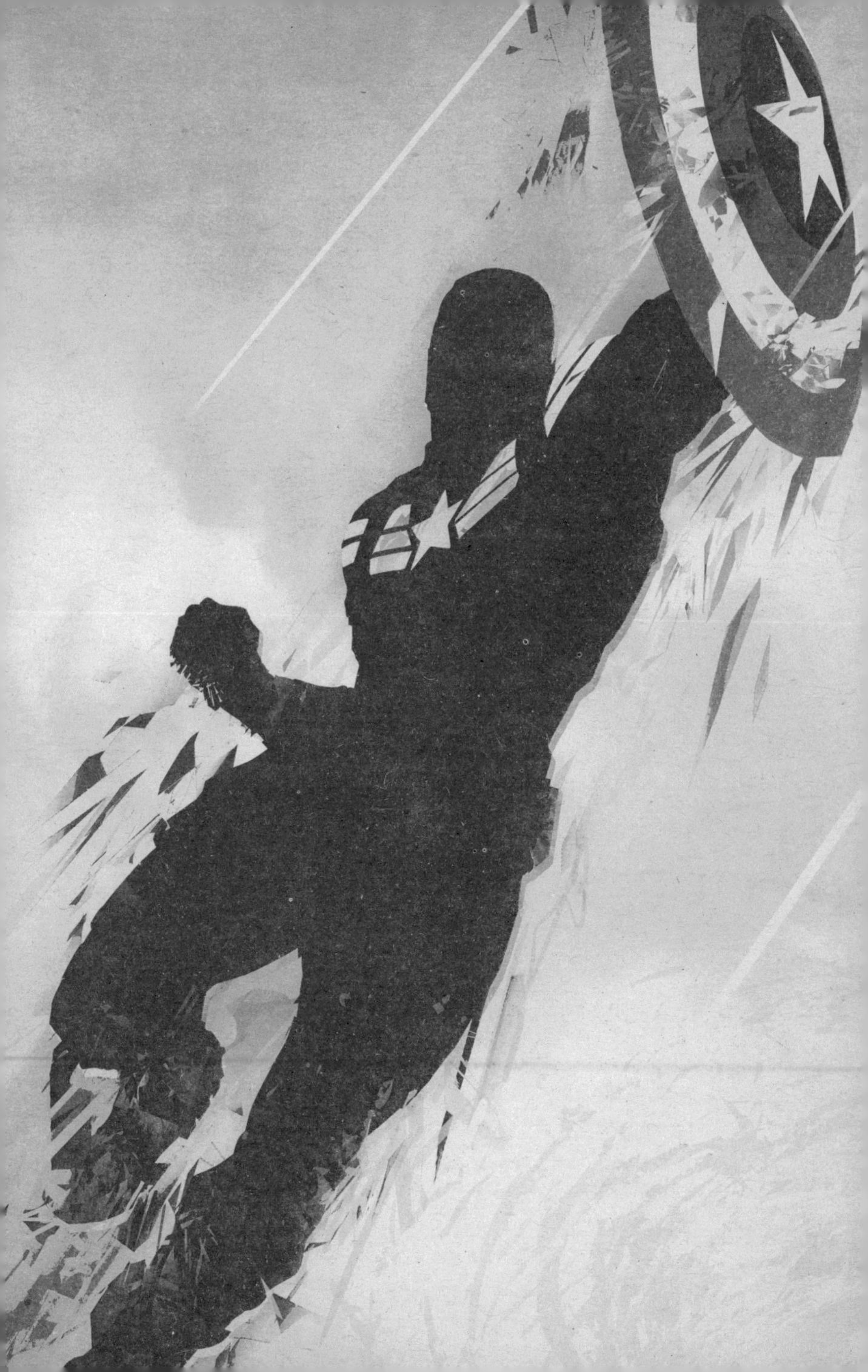

PARAMS-4T_8908-4516FFK-3-TAKK-90
3K_HJ041556-0-5PD043099-168-ABLZ
TERS-32-89-JKLBD_89021-JK05-4-465

FIRST ENCOUNTER

THE FIRST TRICKLES of morning
light reflected on the Washington Monument, casting
shadows over the city. As the people of Washington,
D.C., awoke from their slumber, Sam Wilson made
his way through the desolate streets. Besides the foot-
steps of this early-riser athlete, a silence enveloped
the political center of the United States of America.

As Sam passed Independence Avenue, he pounded
by the Capitol, which gleamed with the first bits of
sunlight. He made his way past the Lincoln Memorial,
where the statue of Honest Abe watched over the city.
But he didn't stop to notice the beauty of the solitude

that morning in D.C. or the famed sights that could easily fill up a tourist's day.

As the morning grew, Sam reached the reflecting pool on the mall, an outdoor area that usually bustled with people but that remained empty in the early morning. The only other person was a solitary runner who moved so fast he appeared almost as a specter or an animal running to catch its prey. Sam watched in awe as the figure came at him.

"On your left!" the runner called out as he zipped past. Sam was determined to catch up. His competitive nature always came out on the running path, wanting to beat others on the road. But this time it wasn't about beating another guy's time; this was about learning the secrets to the magician's tricks.

But the other runner passed him again. And again. It felt as if he was making loops just to intimidate Sam, who was becoming even more determined to catch up.

As he passed him again, the runner called out, "On your left!"

Sam picked up his speed, his feet pounding against the pavement, running as fast as he could, panting and pushing himself harder and faster until finally he was forced to stop for breath. His lungs burned and grasped for oxygen. Sweat dripped down his face. Sucking in air and trying to bring his heart rate down, he sat in the grass, depleted.

"Do you need a medic?"

An exhausted Sam looked up at a man who stood with great stoic presence. Taking in a deep breath, he replied, "I think I need a new set of lungs."

Sam's shirt was drenched in sweat. Shocked, he noticed the runner's bone-dry sweatshirt. Was this guy human? How could he run that fast and not even break a sweat? Impossible, he thought.

When he caught his breath, he said, "Dude, I think you just did thirteen miles in thirty minutes."

"Got a late start," the runner replied.

"Really? What happens when you are on time? You get home before you leave?" he asked, almost joking.

The man helped Sam to his feet and looked at his National Guard sweatshirt. "What group were you with?" he asked proudly.

"Fifty-eighth pararescue," Sam stated. "But I'm working at the V.A. now. You?"

"Army," the man replied.

The army? Sam thought. "Where'd you serve?"

"Europe, mostly."

Sam gulped. America hadn't been at war in Europe since the 1940s. And then it hit him. The runner had to be the world-famous Captain America.

With a gleam of recognition in his eyes, he questioned Cap. "Really, when?"

Cap realized the soldier had it figured out. His cover was blown. He extended his hand. "Steve Rogers."

Impressed, Sam shook Steve's hand and introduced himself. "Sam Wilson."

Then Sam stood silently, staring at the military celebrity. It was a meeting he would never have imagined when he'd left his house that morning.

"I read about you. The whole defrosting thing.

Must be weird. I mean . . . I was only gone for four years," Sam said. He was both in awe of and sympathetic to the life of a soldier away from home.

"I watch a lot of History Channel. Been reading the Internet, you know? To catch up," Steve replied.

"The whole thing?" Sam questioned.

"There are a lot of pictures," Steve retorted.

It couldn't be that easy, Sam thought. Even as Captain America, Steve couldn't easily adjust to life half a century into the future. It hadn't been a breeze for Rip Van Winkle. And truthfully, it hadn't been that easy for Sam Wilson, either. When he came back to the States after serving four years in Afghanistan, readjusting to society was an extremely difficult task. It's never an easy adjustment to civilian life.

"You missed, like, half the twentieth century. All I missed was the last season of *Lost*," Sam said to Steve, but he could tell that Steve didn't get the *Lost* reference. "It's a TV show," he clarified.

"I'll put it on the list," Steve replied.

Sam snickered, thinking he was making a joke, but then Steve actually pulled a small pad out of his pocket to make a note. Like his shirt, the pad was completely dry despite his long run. Sam looked over, wondering what Steve thought he had missed when he was frozen in ice: Soundgarden, Thai food, *Star Wars*, to name a few.

Then Steve's cell phone chirped. He looked at the message: CRIMSON ALERT. EXTRACTION IMMINENT.

He shook Sam's hand. "Looks like they need me to work, but nice to meet you, Sam."

Sam didn't want the encounter to end and said, "If you ever want to drop by the V.A., make me look completely awesome in front of the girl at the desk, let me know."

"I'll keep it in mind," Steve said with a smile.

Suddenly, a sports car pulled up and an attractive woman with dark hair and sunglasses popped her head out the driver's-side window.

She asked the men, "Do either of you know where the Smithsonian is? I'm here to pick up a fossil."

Sam looked past her to the museum, which was just across the street. *Does she not see it right there?* he thought.

PBRRM3-4T-8908-431GFFK-3-THCK-90
3K-HJ841556-0-SPB843098-168-RBLZ
TLRS-32-B0-JKLUD-89821-JKR5-4-765

The woman stepped out of the sleek sports car and smiled, taking off the wig and shaking her luxurious real red hair, revealing her true identity: Natasha Romanoff, otherwise known as S.H.I.E.L.D. agent and super spy Black Widow.

Natasha looked at Sam, acknowledging him with a casual "Hey."

"Hi," he replied, staring at the scene before him, trying to make sense of everything.

Steve smiled and got into the sports car with Natasha. "You can't run everywhere," he said to Sam. Then they peeled off, leaving a cloud of dust behind them.

BRIEFING #3

HOSTAGES
AND HARD DRIVES

THE QUINJET flew high above the Indian
Ocean, lurking in the clouds like a ghost, quiet but
present. Inside the state-of-the-art S.H.I.E.L.D. jet,
Steve Rogers was suited up in Captain America's
stealth suit, which he wore when in the midst of a
serious undercover operation.

He huddled with Black Widow and the
S.T.R.I.K.E. team while the squad's leader, Brock
Rumlow, updated them on their latest mission, show-
ing them a monitor displaying images of an enormous
aircraft carrier with a large launching pad.

Brock pointed to the screen. "The target's a mobile
satellite launch platform called the *Lemurian Star*. They

were about to send up their last payload when pirates took her over. That was ninety-three minutes ago."

"Any demands?" Captain America asked.

"A billion and a half," Rumlow replied.

Captain America was shocked by the amount of ransom they were demanding for a boat. Pirates attacked all the time and never demanded a billion dollars in ransom. In the 1940s that would have been an inconceivable figure, and it was extremely high even by modern standards.

"Why so steep?" Cap had to know.

"'Cause it's S.H.I.E.L.D.'s. . . ."

Captain America frowned. How had S.H.I.E.L.D. let this happen? Their ships weren't supposed to be this vulnerable. Now he understood why the criminals could ask for so much money. Cap studied the map and realized the ship was in dangerous waters. No wonder it had been captured! "So it's not off course, it's trespassing."

Then Black Widow came to S.H.I.E.L.D.'s defense. "I'm sure they have a very good reason."

Captain America frowned. "I'm getting a little tired of being Fury's janitor." To him, it seemed like he was always cleaning up messes that S.H.I.E.L.D. got itself into.

"Relax. This one's not that complicated," Black Widow said, attempting to soothe the First Avenger.

But Captain America focused on the reality of the mission, pointing to satellite photos of armed men patrolling the deck.

"How many pirates?" Cap asked Rumlow.

"At least fifteen." Rumlow brought up an image of a man on the monitor. "Group of top mercs led by this guy, Georges Batroc, ex-DGSE—French Government Agency—action division. He notched thirty-six kill missions."

The team looked at pictures of Batroc in Serbia as Rumlow filled them in on his criminal past.

"The hostages?" Captain America asked when Rumlow was finished.

Rumlow pulled up the hostages' photos. They were all S.H.I.E.L.D. ID photos, including those of the ship's crew. Rumlow told them, "They're mostly techs. One officer. Jasper Sitwell. They're holding them in the galley."

Captain America studied the ship's layout. Something doesn't make sense, he thought. What's Sitwell doing on a launch ship? He knew there was a vital piece of information he was missing. They asked him to save the day but never told him why.

Within seconds he had a plan in place. "I'll clear the deck, then find Batroc," he told the others. Then he turned to Black Widow. "Find the hostages. Get them to the life pods. Get them out."

Rumlow was eager to follow Captain America's plan. "S.T.R.I.K.E. team, gear up."

"You do anything Saturday?" Black Widow queried Cap.

"Do sit-ups count?" Cap didn't like people asking about his personal life. He knew what Black Widow was implying, but he wasn't looking for a date.

"You and I have had a lot of free time since New York City. You might want to leave the house for some of it. You know Kristen. The girl in statistics?

She would so say yes if you asked her out."

"I don't date at work."

"That makes it tough when you never stop working."

Captain America just wanted Black Widow to drop the subject. "Schedule's a little tight these days."

Suddenly, a red light went on, and the Quinjet's back hangar doors opened. A strong wind whipped through the hull and Steve yelled over the noise, "See? No time!"

He raced the length of the jet and leaped out the door. The S.T.R.I.K.E. agents started to follow but stopped when they realized Cap was missing something!

"Was he wearing a parachute?" an agent called out.

"No," Rumlow confirmed. "No, he wasn't."

Steve hurtled headfirst, like a missile, out of the Quinjet and toward the *Lemurian Star*. At the last moment, he flipped and landed in the water, less than a hundred yards from the ship.

The huge satellite platform floated in the calm

water, with the reflection of the moonlight on its deck. A half-assembled rocket stood under a scaffold on the port side.

Suddenly, a pirate standing guard was taken by surprise by Captain America, who silently emerged from the water and grabbed his ankles, disposing of the goon with perfect strikes. In the pitch-dark night in the middle of the sea, Cap parkoured his way across the deck with ease, taking out another pirate, making it seem almost effortless.

Several more pirates patrolled the deck. But they were no match for the Super-Soldier! Emerging from the shadows with a stealthy attack, he dispensed of them all in short order. Cap thought he had the last pirate pinned to the deck when he turned to see another pointing a gun to his head.

Captain America quietly whispered into his ear communicator, "Clear." And the pirate was safely taken out, thanks to Rumlow who was perched on a nearby tower. Above Rumlow, Black Widow and four more skydivers in stealth gear slapped their chest releases, and their chutes billowed into the night as they fell to the deck, rolled, then popped up, sidearms in hand. Cap ran toward the side of the carrier with Black Widow by his side. They were taking back this boat, and the hostages.

Captain America was hyper-focused on the rescue of the hostages, but Black Widow was still in the middle of the conversation he'd believed was over. "What about that nurse who lives across the hall from you? She seems nice."

She wouldn't give up! He'd jumped out of the Quinjet without a parachute to avoid her, but she didn't get the hint. Truthfully, he'd jumped out of the Quinjet to save the hostages, but he seriously didn't want to hear another comment about his dating life, or the lack of one.

"Secure the engine room. Then find me a date," he replied flatly.

"I'm multitasking," she replied as she expertly slipped through a nearby hatch, disappearing.

Cap finally reached the com tower. He climbed halfway up a large gas line pipe, then removed a small surveillance launcher from his pouch and fired it at the bridge. It arced through the air and stuck to the window of the com tower. Instantly, Cap heard static, so he used his hands to cover his ears so he could hear.

He could make out Batroc, who was speaking in French. Luckily, Cap spoke the language as well! He learned that Batroc was calling down to the engine room.

"I want this ship ready to move when the ransom comes," Batroc informed the group and then he hung up.

The pirate on the other end of the line hung up the phone but was immediately kicked to the ground by Black Widow, who descended on a zip line. She stunned another pirate using her Widow's Bite bracelets. Two pirates looked up but before they could react, Black Widow flipped with ease and descended on top of them, taking them out with precision strikes. Looking around at the fallen goons, she smirked. Child's play, she thought.

Meanwhile, the hostages, including Officer Jasper Sitwell, were bound and kept in the galley. They were made to sit on the floor while being guarded by a band of armed pirates. It was a tense scene.

The hostages weren't the only folks growing tired of the situation. "I need a break. Go find Jacques," one of the pirates demanded of another.

"I'll get him," the second pirate replied, but he didn't make it very far. As he turned the corner, he ran right into Rumlow and his energy truncheon! *ZAP!* The pirate began to stagger back, but Rumlow grabbed him before he banged against the galley door, and then quietly laid him on the floor for a nice long nap.

Rumlow listened for other pirates. When he saw that all was clear, he pressed a metal disk to the door, locking it down.

Back in a lower part of the ship, Black Widow spoke into her earpiece and let Captain America know that the engine room was secure. She had taken out all the pirates.

Just then, Captain America, Rumlow, and a band of S.T.R.I.K.E. snipers blew open the door to the galley. As they burst into the room, S.H.I.E.L.D. Officer Sitwell knew he was saved. "I told you," he said to the pirates who lowered their weapons in fear. "S.H.I.E.L.D. doesn't negotiate." Knowing the hostages were secured, Cap went after Batroc.

But Batroc could sense he was in trouble. He heard one of the pirates talking over the radio, worried that he'd lost contact with the galley. But Batroc had more to worry about than the hostages.

Suddenly, Captain America burst into the control room! But there was no Batroc. He alerted Black Widow. "Batroc's on the move. Circle back to Rumlow and protect the hostages." But there was no answer. "Natasha?"

Out of nowhere, a booted foot kicked Cap in the head. *Whack!* Batroc pounced just as Cap managed to get his shield up. Batroc unleashed a fury of punches and kicks, driving Steve back. Taken by surprise, Cap got into a battle stance, ready for a fight.

"Stop kicking me!" he shouted to Batroc, and with his superhuman strength he threw Batroc through a door.

PARAM3-4T_8900-45IGFFK-3-THKK-98
3K_HJ041556-0-5PBD43899-L60-A8LZ
ILRS-32-89-JKLOU_89B21-JK85-4-465

Batroc groaned and then passed out. Captain America looked up and saw Black Widow at a computer.

"What are you doing?" Cap asked.

"Backing up the hard drive. It's a good habit to get into."

"I told you to find Rumlow. What are you doing here?"

Black Widow didn't pay any attention to Cap's query and swiveled to another monitor. Captain America looked over her shoulder.

"You're saving S.H.I.E.L.D. intel," he said, his tone almost questioning.

Captain America was lost when it came to modern technology. Black Widow frowned at the screen as a red file icon pulsed: LOCKED.

"Our mission is to rescue *hostages*," Cap said with intensity, still focused on finishing the job.

Black Widow inserted a translucent S.H.I.E.L.D. data drive into the computer. "That's your mission."

Over the intercom Rumlow made an announcement: "All hostages are secure."

"And you handled it beautifully." Black Widow yanked the hard drive out of the computer. "See? No mess."

A noise came from the floor and they looked down to see a hand grenade rolling toward them. Cap whirled to see Batroc escaping.

The Super-Soldier flipped the grenade with his shield, simultaneously tossing Black Widow and himself toward a nearby glass partition. They smashed through as the explosion tore the computer room to shreds. A fireball rocketed down the steel corridor that Cap and Black Widow now raced down, his shield protecting her from the flames and debris.

When the dust and debris settled and all was quiet, Black Widow looked at Cap and said, "And *that's* why you back up your hard drive."

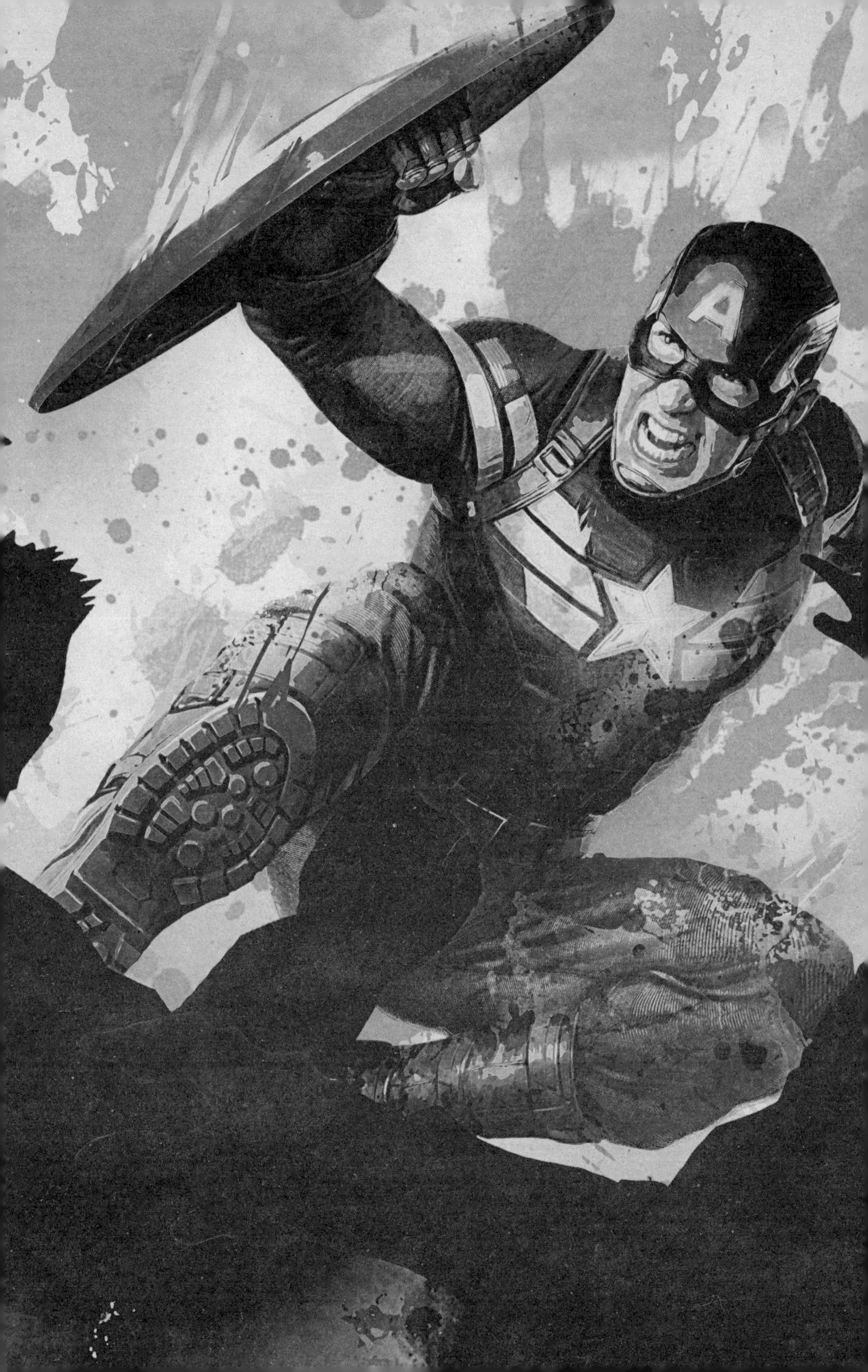

BRIEFING #4

WHAT'S IN THE PAPER BAG?

S.H.I.E.L.D. HEADQUARTERS loomed over Washington, D.C.'s Potomac River. Although the building sat on the edge of still waters, inside it was a bustling center of activity for its elite team of agents.

In Nick Fury's sleek, ultra-high-tech office, Steve Rogers stood looking down at Fury, who sat at his desk. Dressed in his stealth suit, Cap glared at S.H.I.E.L.D.'s director. "You just can't stop yourself from lying, can you?"

Nick Fury defended himself. "I didn't lie. Agent Romanoff just had a different mission than you."

With a slight attitude, Steve leaned in and retorted, "Which you didn't feel obliged to share."

"I'm not obliged to do anything."

"Those hostages could have died," Rogers explained, visibly upset that Natasha's main focus wasn't the hostages but the hard drive. Wasn't Fury upset about the *Lemurian Star* being taken over by pirates? There had been a S.H.I.E.L.D. officer aboard that carrier. Didn't Fury have a conscience?

"I sent the greatest soldier in history to see that they didn't."

This statement didn't stroke Steve Rogers's ego. He stared down Fury. He was genuinely annoyed and Fury could tell. "Soldiers trust one another. That's what makes it an army. Not a bunch of guys running around."

But Fury wouldn't give Steve the last word, saying, "Last time I trusted anyone, I lost an eye." Then he paused. "Look, I didn't want you to do anything you weren't comfortable with. And agent Romanoff is comfortable with everything."

"I can't lead a mission if the people I'm leading have a mission of their own." Steve wasn't taking any excuses from Fury. He'd had enough of being kept in the dark. He'd told Natasha that he was tired of cleaning up Fury's messes and he meant it.

"It's called compartmentalizing. Nobody spills the secrets because nobody knows them all," Fury told Steve.

"Except you," Steve replied.

"But I do share," Fury said with a devious smirk. "I'm nice like that."

Cap was confused. What did Fury mean? Then the director of S.H.I.E.L.D. stood and walked out of his office, motioning for Steve to follow. The conversation wasn't over. As they headed into an elevator, a sensor detected both men.

"Insight Bay," Fury called out to the sensor.

"Captain Rogers does not have clearance for that sector," a computerized voice announced.

"Director override, Fury, Nicholas J.," he ordered the computer.

Although Steve had been unfrozen for some time, he was still adjusting to the modern world. Even a ride in an elevator seemed strange compared to when he used to ride them back in the forties. "They used to play music," he said to Fury.

"I know. My grandfather operated one for forty years."

This wasn't your typical elevator. It was made of glass, and the D.C. skyline was visible. Maybe there wasn't piped-in music, but a tourist would definitely break out a camera to take a picture of the view.

Fury continued, "Granddad worked in a nice building. Made good tips. Walked home every night with a roll of dollars wrapped in his lunch bag. He'd say hi; people would say hi back. Time went by. The neighborhood got tougher. He'd say hi. They'd say, 'Keep walkin'.' He got to gripping that lunch bag pretty tight."

The view of D.C. turned black as the walls of the elevator shaft came into play. The car descended under the streets at an accelerated rate. They had to be more than a thousand feet belowground.

"He ever get mugged?" Steve asked.

"Every week some punk wanted to know what was in the bag," Fury said.

"What would he do?"

"He'd show 'em a handful of dollars and a glimpse of his gun." Fury added with a grin, "Granddad loved people, but he sure didn't trust them very much."

The elevator finally came to a stop and the doors hissed open. Steve stared past Fury, stunned at what he saw. Three massive Helicarriers stood before him. What was S.H.I.E.L.D. making? And was he a part of it?

"I know. They're a little bigger than my grand-dad's gun."

Steve was speechless, focusing on the airships. They were sleeker and more menacing than the old one he had once called home with his fellow Avengers. But that older model was being decommissioned. As they walked beneath the new Helicarriers, Fury clued Steve in on the latest information about them.

"Project: Insight. Luxor class. Synced to a network of target satellites," Fury explained.

It was all beginning to make sense. Now Steve knew why the pirates had taken over the S.H.I.E.L.D. carrier. "The targeting satellites launched from the *Lemurian Star.*"

Fury added, "Once we get them in the air, they never need to come down. Continuous suborbital flight courtesy of the new repulsor engines."

Steve had a hunch who was behind this new technology. "Stark?"

"He had a few suggestions after he got up close and personal with our old turbines," Fury said, referring to Iron Man's close encounter with a Helicarrier engine, courtesy of the Asgardian Loki.

As they walked the gangway, Steve eyed the weapons on the deck. The targeting hub, a clear large sphere, bulged below, thousands of little needlelike weapons bristling out of it.

"You are going to need one heck of a paper bag," Steve remarked.

Fury clarified. "The unibeam system can eliminate a thousand individual targets per minute. The

PARRMS-41 8988-45TG6FFK-3-TRKK-98
5K-HJ847556-0-5P0043B99 L60-R8LZ
TLBS-32-89-JKLD0 D9B21-JK85-4-465

tech can read a terrorist's DNA before he even steps out of his spider hole." Fury turned to Steve with determination. "We will be able to neutralize threats before they even start."

Steve didn't like the sound of what S.H.I.E.L.D. was planning. It didn't seem ethical to him. You didn't target people who hadn't done anything wrong.

"Doesn't the punishment usually come after the crime?" he asked innocently.

"We can't afford to wait that long."

"Who's 'we'?" Steve questioned.

"After the events in New York, I convinced the World Security Council that we needed a quantum surge in threat analysis. For once, we're getting ahead of the curve."

They were all shell-shocked after the Battle of New York but this was taking it too far. Steve was getting angry. "By holding a gun to everyone on Earth? It's been tried before. You know how it works out. I joined S.H.I.E.L.D. to protect people, not threaten them."

"I've read the Special Scientific Reserve files. The greatest generation did some pretty mean stuff," Fury said with a glare.

"We *compromised*. Sometimes in ways that didn't let us sleep so great. But we did it so people could be free," Steve said as he turned to the Helicarriers and pointed. "This isn't freedom. It's fear."

"S.H.I.E.L.D. takes the world as it is. Not as we'd like it to be. It's getting damn near past time that you get with the program . . . Captain."

"Don't hold your breath." Steve wasn't taking part in this type of military strategy. Sure an army should be prepared, but this was not typical. Not typical at all.

Steve walked away in disgust as Fury just stood silently.

From his office window, Fury watched Cap drive away from the S.H.I.E.L.D. offices on his beloved motorcycle. He felt the weight of Natasha's data drive in his hand. With a heavy sigh he knew that the fate of the world was in his fingertips.

Fury called out, "Secure office."

Suddenly, the windows went black. Metal shields dropped over the doors. Fury inserted the drive into his computer.

A computerized voice boomed, "Welcome, Director Fury."

"Open *Lemurian Star* satellite launch files," Fury told the voice-activated computer.

"Access denied."

"Run encryption." Fury was annoyed.

"Encryption failed," the monotone voice from the computer informed him.

Growing even more infuriated, he said, "Director override, Fury, Nicholas J."

"Override denied. All files—sealed."

"By whose authority?" Fury asked the machine.

"By Fury, Nicholas J."

Fury stared at the flashing "locked" computer file logo. This wasn't good. This wasn't good at all.

THE AMERICAN DREAM

ALTHOUGH THE WORLD once believed Steve Rogers had perished during World War II, America had not forgotten him. He was still a hero and epitomized the heart of the American soldier.

"Welcome to the Smithsonian Air and Space Museum," a woman said as she guided a class of children down a long corridor in the wing devoted to Captain America.

For Steve Rogers, waking up in the twenty-first century after being frozen for seventy years was a challenge, but seeing the impact his life had had on the world at large was simply surreal.

Just outside the Captain America Wing, a line of kids snaked through the room and under an archway. When they turned a corner, they smiled and giggled with glee. One whispered, "This is it!"

Dozens of tourists crowded around the red, white, and blue memorabilia of America's greatest soldier. In the center of the room was a mural depicting Captain America saluting. It was the crowning jewel of the exhibit. A little boy stood in front of it, looking up at his hero. With a smile, he raised his right hand and saluted back.

In the Captain America Exhibit, the *Spirit of St. Louis,* the plane Charles Lindbergh flew on the first nonstop flight from New York to Paris, hung from the ceiling. "The Star-Spangled Man," Cap's theme song from the forties, blasted into the vast hall. In the corner of the room, Steve slunk past in a low-brimmed hat. He didn't want to be seen, for obvious reasons.

A deep voice came to life over the loudspeakers: "A symbol of hope to the nation. A hero to the world. Captain America represented mankind's most notable attributes."

Giggling kids measured their height against a skinny Steve Rogers exhibit. It showed them that it didn't matter what size you were; it only mattered if you had good intentions.

The voice continued: "Denied enlistment due to poor health, Steve Rogers was chosen for a program unique in the annals of American warfare. One that would transform him into the world's first Super-Soldier."

Steve listened. Hearing his story was one thing. Living through it was another. Steve remembered that day when his entire world changed.

As Steve continued to listen, one of the kids turned to see him taking in the display. The child squinted to get a better look at the man. And then his mouth fell open. The kid raised his hand and attempted to salute his now real idol, Captain America. But Steve raised a finger to his lips as if to say that, yes, he was Captain America, but they should keep it a secret.

Steve quietly moved on to the next "chapter" in his life, one that he remembered all too well. A mannequin in Steve's old uniform with the triangular shield and leather jacket was seen leading his comrades-in-arms up an artificial hill.

"Battle tested, Captain America and his Howling Commandos quickly earned their stripes," the mechanized voice said. "Their mission: taking down HYDRA, the Nazi rogue-science division."

Steve moved on. It was surreal to be there, his life unfolding before his very eyes. Memories he would never forget, now shared with world. People pointed and took pictures with their phones. Some posed with a Cap statue. Funny, he thought. If they only knew that the real Captain America was right behind them!

Steve's smile quickly left as he approached the next piece of his life. A picture displayed a skinny Steve and his best friend, Bucky, arm in arm, smiles on their faces. Happier times.

As the narrator told the story of Steve and Bucky, Steve felt like someone was punching him in the chest. Some memories were just too painful. "Best friends since childhood, James Buchanan Barnes and Steve Rogers were inseparable in both the schoolyard and on the battlefield. Now, after Captain America's miraculous return years later, Barnes is left as the only Howling Commando to give his life in service of his country."

Steve grimaced as he recollected Bucky's final moments on that speeding train in Germany. The Red Skull's men had set up a trap to catch Captain America and Bucky, and Bucky was outnumbered against the technologically advanced HYDRA soldiers. He was injured and fell from the train before Cap could reach him. Steve sighed. In that moment, he wasn't good enough. Wasn't fast enough. Wasn't super enough. And he vowed never to be that weak again.

Steve touched the photo and the plaque that read A FALLEN COMRADE before moving on to the final room. There were no statues or red, white, and blue shields in the last one. There were no plaques or war scenes unfolding on a plastic battlefield. Instead there was a large TV monitor. Shaky black-and-white footage showed Steve and Bucky behind the lines, light-hearted. Steve studying a field map in the snow. The Howling Commandos trudging through the trenches.

Then Steve's heart skipped a beat when he saw

Peggy Carter's face on the screen. Pride had cast a shadow over Steve's earlier life as Captain America. He had protected his country but missed the opportunity to tell the woman of his dreams that he loved her.

"That was a difficult winter," Peggy informed the interviewer in her English accent.

Steve had seen pictures of her since he'd been revived, but it had been so long since he'd heard her voice. He stood, transfixed by her interview, which was dated 1953. Her title was at the bottom of the screen: Lieutenant Corporal Peggy Carter, SSR.

Seated in uniform, Peggy said, "We were in Russia. A blizzard trapped half our battalion behind enemy lines. Steve—Captain America—fought his way through a HYDRA brigade that had pinned the Allies down for months. He saved a thousand men." Peggy started to choke up. "Including the man who would become my husband."

Steve sat down on a bench and pulled out a tarnished, dented compass. He opened it to Peggy's yellowed picture as her interview continued: "Even after he died, Steve was still changing my life."

The reporter prompted her. "I understand you were the last person to speak to Captain Rogers. Before his plane went down . . ."

There was a silence and Steve looked up to see if the interview was over. It wasn't. Peggy just stared at the reporter for a long moment.

She finally replied, "I was."

The reporter asked, "Could you tell us about what he said?"

Steve stared at the flickering face. Peggy looked down into her cup of tea, never answering.

Steve almost let a tear slip out. Only he knew that she'd asked him on a date. He wished he could meet her at the Stork Club like he'd promised, but nobody could see the future. It was tragic to see your past on display in a museum. It made him feel like a dinosaur, a relic. He just didn't fit in. But at least he could still save people. Helping others was a timeless pursuit.

After a long run, fellow soldiers SAM WILSON and STEVE ROGERS take a breather and get to know each other.

Their talk is cut short when super spy and S.H.I.E.L.D. agent NATASHA ROMANOFF pulls up and informs Steve they have a "situation."

Now in his stealth suit, CAPTAIN AMERICA jumps into action to handle the hostage crisis aboard the *Lemurian Star*.

Cap is joined by S.H.I.E.L.D. agent and leader of S.T.R.I.K.E., BROCK RUMLOW.
They devise a plan to take back the ship.

GEORGES BATROC wants a hefty ransom for the hostages he is holding.
But S.H.I.E.L.D. does not negotiate!

After taking out several of Batroc's goons, it's time for CAPTAIN AMERICA to stop Batroc!

While Cap's mission is to save hostages, BLACK WIDOW has her own: save the S.H.I.E.L.D. intel from the ship's computer mainframe.

Back at Nick Fury's office, the **DIRECTOR OF S.H.I.E.L.D.** informs Steve that the *Lemurian Star* was about the hostages—and saving top secret information.

S.H.I.E.L.D.'s next mission is called **PROJECT INSIGHT.** It involves stopping future attacks BEFORE they happen. This upsets Steve. He thinks it is immoral.

While Fury thinks about Project Insight, **HIS SUV IS ATTACKED!**

A MASKED FIGURE armed with heavy weaponry approaches the wrecked SUV. But Fury escapes during the attack!

The mysterious figure known as the **WINTER SOLDIER** watches his reign of destruction unfold before him. Next up: Captain America!

With the recent events involving Fury and the Winter Soldier and his mercenaries terrorizing D.C., **CAP WILL NEED A LITTLE HELP** to stop this latest threat.

When Sam Wilson hears that Captain America is in trouble and needs help, he answers the call by telling Cap about his **EXO-7 FALCON SUIT!**

BRIEFING #6
AVENGERS: ASSEMBLE

"I still believe in heroes."

—Nick Fury

CAPTAIN AMERICA had a lot of catching up to do. He was still trying to adjust to a world with television and one without the Dodgers playing baseball in Brooklyn. But Nick Fury wasn't going to give the iconic hero time to reflect; he wanted him to soldier on and join a team he was creating. A team that would bring together a group of remarkable people so that when the world needed them, they could fight the battles that the people of Earth couldn't. It was called the Avengers Initiative.

Fury invited Cap aboard the S.H.I.E.L.D. Quinjet. He asked him to help S.H.I.E.L.D. stop the Asgardian Loki, Thor's trickster brother, who had stolen the Tesseract, an ancient crystal-like cube that had the power to destroy the earth, and some say the universe. Loki was planning to harness the energy from the Tesseract to launch a full-scale attack on New York City.

The Avengers were made up of Super Heroes Thor, Hulk, Iron Man, and agents Black Widow, Hawkeye, and now . . . Captain America. Some members of the elite team felt Captain America wasn't ready for the battle. They believed, because he had been frozen for so long, he'd lost his edge. Also, he came from another time period, one that was very simple.

Steve Rogers had serious issues with one Avenger: billionaire-genius Tony Stark, also known as Iron Man. Although Steve knew Tony's father, Howard, who had been there when Cap was transformed into a Super-Soldier, and later made him his famed vibranium shield, these two Super Heroes always seemed to be in the middle of a fight. Anytime Steve spoke,

PARAM3-4T_8900-45TGFFK-3-THKK-90
5K_HJ041556-0-5P0043899-L68-RRLZ
TLR5-32-89-JKL00_09821-JK05-4-465

Tony had a witty retort. Steve followed orders, while following orders was not Tony's thing. But one thing they did agree on was stopping Loki.

Although the Avengers were no strangers to battling villains, Loki's alien army was a fight they couldn't have imagined. The intensity of the attack was exhausting and there were times when they thought they might not be able to save the day. Loki unleashed numerous aliens on flying chariots and creatures that shot through the skies high above the city. The trickster used the Tesseract, perched atop Stark Tower, to open a portal where the aliens emerged. It seemed like there was a never-ending army of aliens called the Chitauri that poured from the portal.

Besides battling heavily armed aliens, the Avengers had to deal with thousands of civilians who were constantly in the way, by no fault of their own. While a few of the Super Heroes battled the Chitauri in the sky, Captain America and Black Widow were on the ground directing "traffic" and getting the innocent out of harm's way. They helped civilians on the streets of New York City, which were littered with debris the alien army had created, leading them to safe areas.

The team continued to fight alongside one another, brothers-in-arms. When one went down, another would help them to their feet. They were a team. They were the Avengers.

But they were overwhelmed. The only way to win was by closing the portal. So when the time came to put an end to the battle, the World Security Council launched a nuclear missile into the heart of Manhattan, which Fury highly advised was something *not* to do. But Iron Man intercepted the missile and decided to take it to the one place where it would detonate in their favor: the Chitauri wormhole.

Iron Man blasted toward the wormhole, pushing his suit to its limits. He made it through to the other side of the wormhole and tossed the missile toward the mother ship. It detonated and destroyed the Chitauri lead ship, leaving their forces disabled on Earth. Stark's suit lost power and fell to Earth but Iron Man was saved by the Hulk. Iron Man could have easily gotten killed. This helped Captain America see a side of Iron Man he hadn't before, and he began to respect Tony for being sacrificial, a true soldier.

Captain America had led a team of Super Heroes against a common enemy and won the battle. But many more battles would be fought. And he was prepared to defend his country and the world.

2-00-5_UUIGGE_67-8900

BRIEFING #7
A FAVOR

FURY STEPPED inside a secure elevator deep below the streets of Washington, D.C. He leaned in to the retina reader, which scanned his good eye. "World Security Council," Fury said.

The elevator doors closed and the machine hummed to life, the car accelerating until he was high above the city.

Almost fifty stories above D.C., a very important meeting was unfolding inside the World Security Council Chambers. Four holograms represented council members from around the world: America, India, China, and Great Britain. All powerful. All with an agenda. All upset with S.H.I.E.L.D.

"This failure is unacceptable," said the Chinese councilman.

The Indian council member folded his hands and leaned in. "Considering the attack took place a mile from my country's sovereign waters, it's a bit more than that. I move for immediate hearings."

"We don't need hearings," said the British council member. "We need action. It's this council's duty to oversee S.H.I.E.L.D. A breach like that raises serious questions."

The American councilman didn't look pleased. "Like how the heck did a French pirate manage to hijack a covert S.H.I.E.L.D. vessel in broad daylight?"

As the four holograms argued about what had occurred with the *Lemurian Star*, the only real human in the room, Secretary Alexander Pierce, cleared his throat. "For the record, councilman, he's Algerian. I can draw a map if it would help."

He gave a wry smile. The other council members became quiet as Pierce continued to hold the floor. "I don't need to remind you that our world, on its best day, is chaotic. And on its worst . . .

worse. If the council intends to fall to rancor every time our mission is tested . . . then maybe we need someone to oversee us. Frankly, despite the size of this facility, I don't think they've got the office space."

The council members frowned. They had been put in their places. But their scolding was interrupted by an assistant who stepped into the room and whispered into Pierce's ear.

"More trouble, Mr. Secretary?" asked the British councilman.

Pierce smiled and stood. "That would depend on your definition."

The secretary stepped out to find Nick Fury waiting for him in the hall. Pierce looked at his old friend. "I work forty floors away and it takes a hijacking for you to visit?"

Fury smiled. "Nuclear war would do it, too."

"What's wrong with Christmas?"

Fury chuckled. "You busy in there?"

"Nothing some earmarks from the discretionary budget can't fix," Pierce said.

Nick Fury turned serious. "I need to ask for a favor and it's not small."

Pierce's smile faded. "I'm listening . . . and I'm nervous."

"I'd like for you to call a vote." Fury's face became tight. He was unsure how Pierce would react. "Project: Insight has to be delayed."

"Delay Insight?" Pierce said with severity in his tone. "That's not a favor, that's a cabinet meeting. A long one."

He wasn't taking it well, so Fury tried to reassure him. "It might be nothing. It probably is nothing. I just need some time to make sure it's nothing."

"But if it's something?" Pierce asked.

Fury sighed. "Then we will both be glad those Helicarriers aren't in the air."

Pierce stared at Fury for a few seconds, considering his request. Finally, he broke the silence. "You're buying me dinner. And not at the S.H.I.E.LD. commissary."

Nick Fury nodded. "Thank you, sir."

Pierce turned to head back into the meeting. "Don't thank me yet."

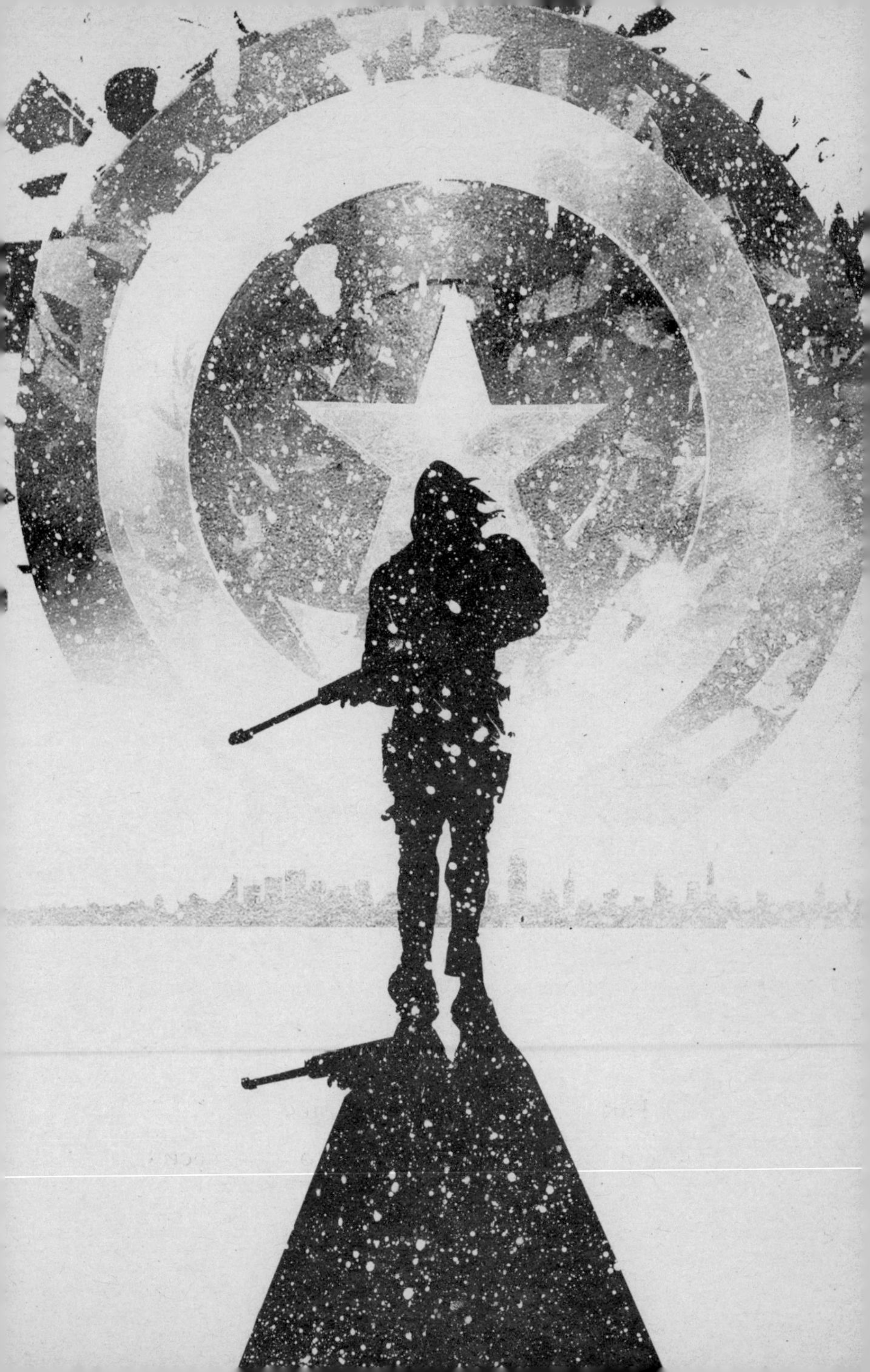

YOU FIGHT FOR US, WE FIGHT FOR YOU

"A COP pulled me over last week. He thought I was drunk," said a woman in the veterans' support group circle. She wrung her hands as Sam listened to every word, nodding for her to continue.

The woman went on. "I swerved to miss a plastic bag. Thought it was an IED. . . in Falls Church, Virginia," she said, referring to an improvised explosive device. She thought about the numerous times her assault vehicle had to swerve to avoid mines that had been planted in the ground, hidden from sight.

Sam nodded again. He understood all too well how this was second nature to her: to avoid and survive. He turned to the group and addressed them.

"The deal is, some stuff we leave there. Other stuff we bring back. Our job is to figure out how to carry it."

Sam noticed Steve slip in through the back door.

"Is it going to be in a big suitcase or a little man purse?" Sam said. "It's up to you. . . ." He thanked the group and the meeting ended.

Steve watched the veterans leave, giving them each a thin smile as Sam approached and said, "Look who it is. The running man."

"Pretty intense," Steve said, referring to the meeting he just saw wrap up. He helped Sam fold up the chairs from the circle.

"Lots of us came back with the same problems, you know? Guilt . . . regret . . ." Sam suddenly became quiet as emotions took over. It was a meeting again, Sam in the circle this time.

Then Steve decided to open up as well. "I grew up with a guy. We grew up together."

Sam knew by the tone in Steve's voice it was someone who had served with him. "He make it back?" Sam asked.

Steve sighed and looked to the floor, pain in his

eyes. "Killed in action." There was silence between them for a few seconds before Steve continued. "I've been through a lot of changes. I don't know if anything hit me as hard as losing Bucky."

"We fight for our guys, ya know?" Sam said, looking into Steve's eyes. He understood. "When they go, a part of us does, too."

"You lose someone?" Steve asked.

"My wingman," Sam replied. "Riley. Flying a night mission. Standard rescue op. Done it a thousand times. Until a rocket-propelled grenade blew Riley out of the sky."

Silence.

Finally, Sam continued. "Couldn't do anything about it. It was like I was just up there to watch."

Steve sighed. Soldiers shared a lot with one another. And often one of those things was losing a friend in battle. "I'm sorry."

"After that I had a real hard time trying to find a reason to be over there."

"And you're happy back in the world?" Steve asked.

"Food's better," Sam joked. "And the number of

people who give me orders is about down to zero. So, yeah." He stacked his last chair and realized this wasn't idle talk. "You thinking of getting out?"

"No . . . I don't know. What would I do with myself if I did?" Steve said, taking in Sam's words.

"Ultimate Fighting? That's just a great idea off the top of my head." He saw that Steve wasn't laughing, so he attempted to be more thoughtful. "Seriously. You could do whatever you wanted. What makes you happy?"

Steve thought for a few seconds. "I don't know."

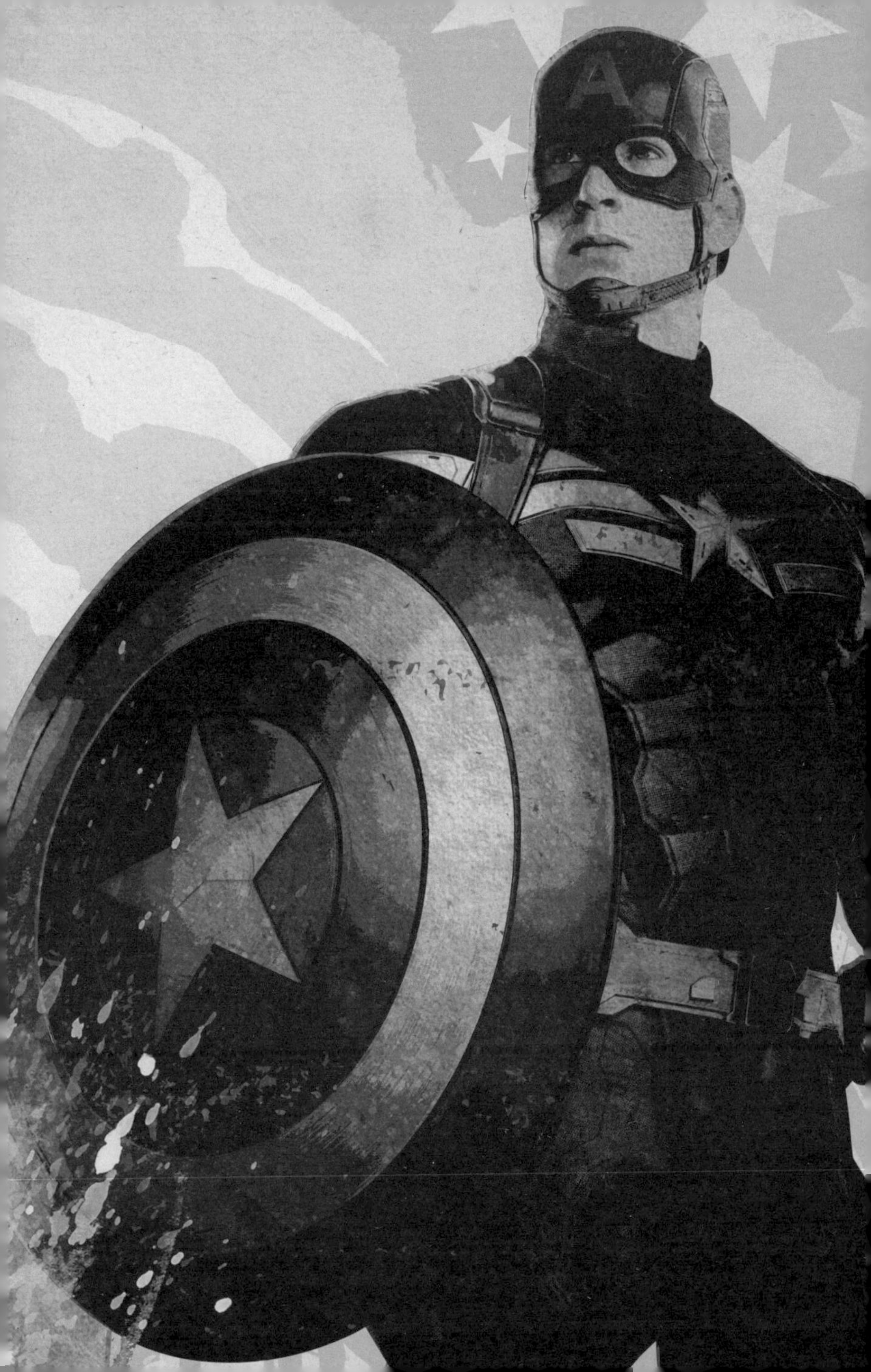

BRIEFING #9
TRAFFIC JAM

WASHINGTON, D.C., passed by in the reflection of Nick Fury's sleek, state-of-the-art black S.H.I.E.L.D. SUV as he drove a little faster than he normally would. A complex Heads-Up Display, or HUD, flashed on his windshield: altitudes, headings, and numerical codes. It read license plates of passing cars. It scanned faces that walked by on the streets, bringing up their entire history right before Fury's eyes. But he paid this unlimited information no mind. He was bothered by Steve's comments back at the Triskelion. Was Steve right? Would more lives be in jeopardy due to Project: Insight?

Fury sighed. Then he spoke to the digital wind-shield. "Open secure line 0405."

A live feed of Nick Fury's second-in-command, Maria Hill, appeared in the corner.

"This is Hill."

"I need you in D.C.," Fury said. "Deep Shadow Conditions."

Hill knew this was serious. "Give me four hours."

"You have three."

Fury hung up the call and stopped at an intersection. A police car pulled up alongside his SUV and the cop leaned in a bit toward Nick. He eyed the officer suspiciously.

"You wanna see the lease?" Fury said nonchalantly.

The cop glared; then his partner picked up a call. Their siren blared and they squealed away. Fury smirked. "Humph."

Suddenly . . .

BAM! A police car smashed into Fury's driver's-side door, causing the SUV to sideswipe a nearby mailbox and crumple a phone pole. Fury, wearing a seat belt, was shaken up but unharmed. He looked around, then, suddenly . . . *BAM!* A second cop car slammed into the SUV, this time from the front. Then a third crashed it from behind. This was an attack!

Fury clawed his way out from behind the air bag that had exploded to protect him. Fractured data splintered across his spider-webbed windshield. Numbers and colors flickered as a warning sign flashed in the corner.

"Ulnar fracture detected," said a computerized voice as an image of Fury's wounded arm appeared on the cracked HUD. A first-aid kit popped out from a hidden console. Fury grabbed a syringe and jabbed it into his arm, helping relieve the immense pain from the fracture, if just for a few minutes. He turned and watched the first cop car screech backward. Was it preparing to ram the SUV—*again?*

Fury braced for impact.

Suddenly, a SWAT van pulled up at his side and full-body-armored police piled out armed with assault rifles. The bulletproof glass cracked as thousands of rounds hammered Fury's window.

"Get us out of here!" Fury demanded.

"Propulsion system offline," the computer replied as the video screen went blank. "Rebooting propulsion system."

Suddenly, the guns stopped firing. Fury caught his breath, but only for a second. Two cops jumped out of the SWAT van and carried a large, menacing device to Fury's SUV. Metallic legs sprang from the device and anchored to the asphalt.

BLAM! A high-tech battering ram smashed into Fury's window.

"Shell integrity at fifty-two percent. Door damaged."

"You think?" Fury fired back at the computer. "How long till propulsion?"

"Calculating."

The futuristic-looking ram hummed as it recoiled back and then violently bashed the window again. *BLAM!*

"Shell integrity at thirty-one percent. Deploying countermeasures—"

"Hold that order!" Fury shouted.

BLAM! The glass splintered. Dozens of cops moved toward the crackling window.

"Shell integrity at nineteen percent. Counter-measures advised," the computer stated.

"Hold," Fury said calmly as he watched the cops close in even more, crowding the driver's window. Facial recognition scans read "Assailants Unknown."

The ram hammered again. *BLAM!!!*

"Shell integrity at one percent. Failure imminent."

"Hold."

The video screen blinked. "Countermeasures enabled."

An assault rifle sprang from the center console and Fury opened fire, shattering the window and pushing back the "cops." He reached for a grenade launcher and blasted the SWAT vehicle, flipping it in the air. The digital HUD within the SUV flickered back to life: "Propulsion reboot complete. Propulsion system online."

"Full acceleration!" Fury cried. The SUV squealed

away, steering itself, which was ideal for Fury since he couldn't see through the splintered windshield anyway.

"Hostiles in pursuit," said the computer as Fury looked back to see the "cops" tearing after him in hot pursuit.

Fury turned back to the HUD. "Initiate vertical takeoff."

"Flight system damaged," the computer responded.

"Then activate guidance cameras and give me the wheel," Fury demanded as he grabbed the wheel. A small video screen rose from the dash. Cameras displayed alternate angles of the car's rear, side, and front views. Fury weaved through the traffic, navigating by the screen.

"Multiple pedestrians, fifty yards."

Fury swerved, laying on the horn. Two cop cars pulled up on either side of him. A gunman leaned out of the squad car and opened fire at his driver's window. Fury dodged the attack and leaned out, punching the gunman, who fell back into his car as the three vehicles, now tightly locked together, barreled down the street. The video monitor blinked as it showed an oncoming intersection just a few hundred feet away.

"Intersection approaching," the computer warned him. "Multiple collisions expected."

Fury slammed on the brakes and sent the two police cars hurtling into the intersection, unable to stop. Their tires screeched as smoke rose from underneath the vehicles. *CLASH!* The cars smashed and flipped into each other, causing traffic to come to a squealing halt.

Fury spun his SUV around a corner. The screen flashed to its rearview angle and showed nothing coming. Fury smiled, momentarily clear. Then, suddenly . . .

"Obstruction ahead. Ninety-five yards. Origin unknown."

Fury's screen snapped back to forward view and revealed a masked man with a high-tech launcher standing in the middle of the road. The assassin fired and a black disk slid into the street.

"Incoming projectile detected."

The disk shot under the SUV and unleashed a

fiery explosion, causing the vehicle to cartwheel and skid down the street. Sparks flew everywhere as Fury shielded his eyes. Finally, the SUV came to a stop upside down with Nick hanging from his seat belt as his screen went dark. In the rearview mirror he saw black combat boots approaching.

His face in shadow, the assassin walked calmly toward the SUV, his boots impacting debris and crunching glass beneath his feet.

Fury desperately reached for the controls on his dash.

The assassin dropped the high-tech launcher and pulled out a pistol and, with his other hand, which was made entirely of metal, wrenched the driver's-side door clean from its frame. But Fury was gone! Inside, a perfect circle glowed green where Fury had sliced a hole in the roof of the SUV and the street below. The assassin stared at the hole . . . listening to the sewers. Fury had escaped. For now . . .

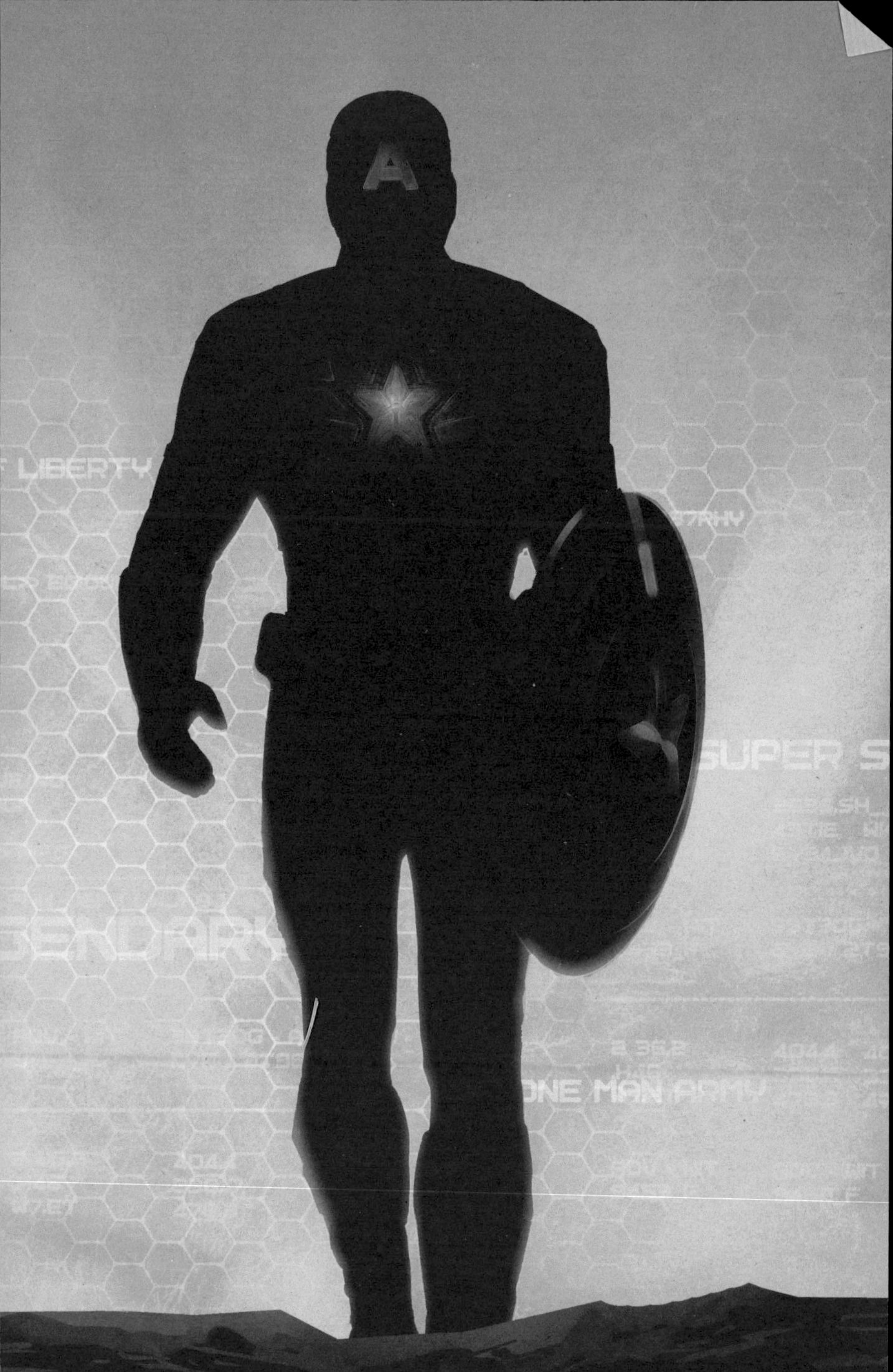
LIBERTY
ONE MAN ARMY

SHOTS FIRED

D.C.'S HISTORIC monuments shined over
the rooftops of the city. It was a quiet night as the
people of the nation's capital settled in. But then a
low rumbling disrupted the peace of a small neighborhood as a motorcycle made its way down an alley
and around a corner. Steve Rogers backed his bike
into a spot and shut the engine off. All was quiet once
again as he made his way into his apartment building.

As he trudged up to the second floor, he ran into
Kate, a rather attractive nurse who lived down the
hall. She was backing out of her apartment carrying
her laundry with a cell phone wedged between an ear
and a shoulder.

"Really?" she said into her phone as she struggled to shut her door. "He did? That's so nice." She noticed Steve and gave him a smile. "I have to go now, though. You sleep well, okay? Don't stay up too late." She hung up the phone. "My aunt," she said. "Kind of an insomniac."

Steve politely nodded. It had been a long day but he didn't want to seem cold.

Kate added, "You're home late." Then her eyebrows went up as she suddenly realized how she sounded. "Not that I'm keeping track of your comings and goings in incredible detail like a stalker."

Steve smiled. "It's just nice someone's paying attention," he said. "You know, if you want . . . you can use my washing machine. It's a little cheaper than the one in the basement."

"Oh, yeah? What's it cost?" she asked with a smile.

He smiled back. Progress. "A . . . cup of . . . coffee?" he said shyly.

Kate grinned. "Thanks, but I already have a load going on downstairs. Besides, you don't want my scrubs in your machine. I just did a rotation in the infectious disease ward."

Steve, again, nodded politely, feeling both disappointed and relieved. "I'll keep my distance."

"Not too far, I hope," she said. After a few seconds, Kate started down the stairs but turned one last time. "By the way, I think you left your stereo on." And then she was gone.

"Right. Thanks," he said, watching her disappear. Then he noticed a lovely 1940s jazz song leaking from under his door.

Steve raced to the hallway window and climbed out onto the fire escape. He headed to his kitchen window, quietly worked it open, and snuck in, moving in silence as the record started over in the background. He grabbed his shield and noticed tiny drops of blood on his floor that led to his living room. He crept toward the couch, where he found a man in the shadows   Nick Fury!

"I don't remember giving you a key," Steve said, lowering his shield.

"You really think I need one?" muttered Fury.

Steve flicked the lights on to see the bruised and battered director of S.H.I.E.L.D. more clearly.

Fury sat up and shut the lights back off.

"That's kind of the problem," Steve retorted as he went to turn the record player off. But Nick motioned to him furiously. Then he raised his cell phone, which read EARS EVERYWHERE.

"I'm sorry," Fury said, giving Steve a wink. "I didn't have anywhere else to crash." He swiped to a new screen that read: S.H.I.E.L.D. COMPROMISED. Then Fury typed: JUST YOU AND ME.

"Just my friends'," Fury said.

"Is that what we are?"

Fury stood. "That's up to y—"

But before he could finish, the window shattered! Someone had fired at Fury! He started to fall, but Steve caught him in midair. "Nick!" He dragged Fury around the corner into the kitchen and looked out the window. There he saw a masked man start to run off. As Steve started to go for the assassin, Fury grabbed his hand and managed to get out a few words:

"Don't . . . trust . . . anyone. . . ." And then he passed out.

Steve opened his hand and saw that Fury had given him a hard drive.

Suddenly, his front door smashed open and Kate burst in, a pistol in her hand.

What the—? Steve was confused.

Kate dropped to Fury's side and put pressure on his wound. "Foxtrot is down and unresponsive," she said into an earpiece. "I need EMTs—"

"Who the heck are you?" Steve said.

"Agent 13. S.H.I.E.L.D. Special Services. I'm assigned to protect you."

"On whose orders?" Steve asked.

She looked down at Fury, who was breathing, but barely. "His," she said.

Her secret ear communicator began to squawk as chatter came over the line until someone finally chimed in, "Do we have a twenty on the shooter?"

Steve whipped back to the window and saw a shadow move across the adjacent roof. "Tell them I'm in pursuit."

And with that, Steve burst through his apartment window, shield first, and went after the masked man. Running along the roof of the bordering building, he leaped across an alley gap and crashed through a window of another building. He tucked, rolled, and popped up, heading into a dead run through a swank office.

He burst through door after door, making his way from one end of the office to the other, with nothing slowing him down. When he broke through the final series of doors and found himself in the office's lobby, a shadow raced over him. He looked up and saw the masked man move past the skylight.

He ran past a set of windows that looked out over the sleeping city. I can't let this menace escape, Steve thought as he ran even faster. He smashed through a door into a conference room at the end of the hall. Through the window he saw the assassin leap down to an adjoining building. Steve took a few steps back and crashed through the conference room window to the lower-level roof. He landed in a roll and when he popped up, he flung his vibranium shield with such

PARAM3-4T_8900-151GFFK-3-THKK-90
3K_HJ041556-0-5P0045099-LG0-A0LZ
ILAS-32-89-JKLDD_09021-JK05-4-465

force the *WHOOSSHH!* could be heard down the block.

One hundred yards before the edge of the roof, the assassin turned, and with a *CLANG!* he plucked Captain America's shield out of the air with ease. Steve just stood there in awe. How could this be? No one had ever done that to his shield. Not Loki. Not the Chitauri. Not even Iron Man!

Then Steve noticed something else. The masked man was holding the shield with an arm that was made entirely of metal! Before Steve could catch his breath and make sense of what was happening, the villain hurled the shield back with such force that when Steve caught it, he skidded back twenty feet.

When Cap finally regained his footing, the assassin was gone. Steve walked to the edge of the building and stared out over D.C. as lights and sirens came from all directions toward his location. Steve sighed. He had failed. He had failed Fury, S.H.I.E.L.D., and the people of his city.

MAN DOWN

A CORVETTE screeched to a halt in front of the hospital located in downtown D.C. A frantic Natasha jumped out. At the door two cops tried to stop her.

"Authorized personnel only, mi—" one of them began. But before he could finish, Natasha flipped him over her hip and took him to the ground with ease. As the other officers drew their sidearms, Agent Sitwell stepped out of the hospital.

"You don't want to do that, officers," he said as Natasha raced past him and into the lobby. She moved down the corridor to the secure emergency unit section and stopped cold. For a moment, she looked lost, alone. Through an observation window, amid a half dozen surgeons, Natasha could make out the pale face of one Nick Fury. She didn't know what to make of it. She could think of more than a hundred reasons this could have happened to Fury. This was someone she looked up to for advice and more. Her mentor. Her friend. Family . . .

She noticed Brock Rumlow whispering into a cell phone off to the side while Steve spoke softly with Maria Hill.

"Is he going to make it?" she asked, steeling herself.

"I don't know," Maria replied, drained from the day's events.

"Tell me about the masked man."

"He was fast," Steve said. "Strong. Had a metal arm."

This struck a chord with Natasha. Metal arm . . .

Natasha turned to Maria. "Ballistics?"

"Three slugs. No rifle. Completely untraceable."

Natasha swallowed hard. "Soviet made?"

"Yes," Maria said, surprised Natasha knew, since Maria was the only one who was supposed to have that information.

Natasha motioned for Steve to join her in the hallway. A deliveryman stocked the gum machine nearby.

"What was Fury doing at your apartment?" She spoke in a low tone.

"I don't know."

"Why are you lying?" she demanded.

Just then Rumlow approached. "Cap. They are asking for you back at S.H.I.E.L.D. headquarters."

Steve nodded and they passed the deliveryman who was stocking the gum. At the open machine, Steve turned back to Natasha. "I'm going to get this guy. I promise."

Steve left Natasha and Brock behind after quickly and quietly placing the hard drive Fury had given him inside the open vending machine in a row of bubblegum. The deliveryman closed the front glass door of the machine and walked away, unaware of Steve's sleight of hand. There sat the S.H.I.E.L.D. data drive. Who would look there? Nobody. And that was exactly what Steve wanted.

STORM THE BASEMENT

SEVERAL HIGH-TECH, fully armed helicopters circled Triskelion on high alert. The director of S.H.I.E.L.D. lay in a hospital in critical condition, and a masked assassin was still on the loose. Who knew what was next? But at least they would be ready. . . .

Steve, now back in his Captain America stealth uniform, exited the elevator and made his way to the director's office. Just as he went to grab the door handle, Agent 13 stepped out. With an awkward glance at Steve, she left. Steve brushed it off and stepped inside. There, looking out over D.C., just like Nick Fury once had, stood Pierce.

"Captain, I'm Alexander Pierce."

Steve stepped up and shook Pierce's hand. "Sir, you were secretary of state under two presidents. I might have been on ice, but I know who you are. It's an honor."

"The honor's mine, Captain. My father served in the 101st."

Steve noticed some photos and walked over to investigate. He stopped in front of a picture of a much younger Nick Fury—with both eyes—his hand on a Bible, being sworn in by Pierce.

"We met five years earlier," Pierce said behind Steve. "I was in the state department in La Paz. Rebels took the embassy. Security got me out, but the rebels took hostages, including my daughter." Pierce led Steve across the office. "Nick Fury was deputy chief of a S.H.I.E.L.D. substation. He came to me with a plan to storm our building through the sewers. I told him, 'No, we'll negotiate.'"

Pierce walked back to the window and looked out. "It turned out they did not negotiate. They gave the kill order, stormed down to the basement"—he turned back to Steve—"and found it empty. Nick had ignored my direct orders. Carried out an unauthorized military operation on foreign soil . . . and saved my daughter's life."

Steve smiled. "So you gave him a promotion."

Pierce nodded and then said, "I need your help, Captain. Nick has left us with certain . . . questions. The first of which is, why did he go to your apartment last night?"

"I'm not sure."

"Did you know it was bugged?"

"I did. Because Fury told me," Steve said.

"Did he tell you he was the one who bugged it?"

Silence fell over the room. And once again, Steve was surprised and confused. What was going on? Why hadn't Fury mentioned that the day before?

Pierce leaned in, sympathetic. "Nick asked me to take the World Security Council job because we were both realists. We knew this job wasn't about ideology. It's about what you have to do right now, today."

"Including listening to me eat breakfast," Steve said, annoyed.

Pierce smiled softly. "I want you to take a look at this." He activated a screen on his wall that displayed S.H.I.E.L.D. agents interrogating Batroc in a gray cell.

Steve couldn't believe it. "This is live?"

Pierce nodded. "They picked him up in a not-so-safe house in Algiers."

"Assassination's not Batroc's line," Steve retorted, referring to Batroc's MO.

"It's more complicated than that." Pierce handed Steve a forensics accounting printout. "Batroc was hired anonymously to attack the *Lemurian Star*. The money went through seventeen fictitious accounts. The last was a holding company registered to a Jacob Veech."

"Am I supposed to know him?" Steve asked as he flipped through the printout.

"Not likely. Veech died six years ago. His last address was 1435 Elmhurst Drive." Pierce stopped and looked at Steve. "When I first met Nick, his mother lived at 1437."

Could the person who hired Batroc be someone who knew Nick? Steve wondered. Could it be possible?

"Half the council thinks it was an excuse to derail Project: Insight. The other half thinks the hijacking was a cover-up for the acquisitions and sales of classified intelligence. That sale went sour," Pierce told Steve. Then he gave a heavy sigh and continued. "You're the last person to see him and I don't think that was an accident. I'm asking you as his friend . . . did he tell you anything that might help us?"

Steve stood there, remembering what Fury had told him in the apartment about trusting people. He thought about what might be on the data drive. He thought about Nick lying in a hospital bed, fighting for his life. He looked at a photo of Nick from when he still had two eyes and then a more recent photo of him glaring from behind his patch. One eye stared at Steve.

"He told me not to trust anyone."

"I wonder if that included him," Pierce replied.

They stared at each other, neither backing down.

Then Pierce said, "You know I'm acting director of S.H.I.E.L.D. I don't ask this lightly."

"I'm sorry, sir. That's all he said." Steve made a move to leave but Pierce's voice stopped him.

"Captain? Understand this: I'm going to use all of the tools of this office to get the person responsible for hurting Fury."

Steve stood stoic. So will I, he thought. So will I. . . .

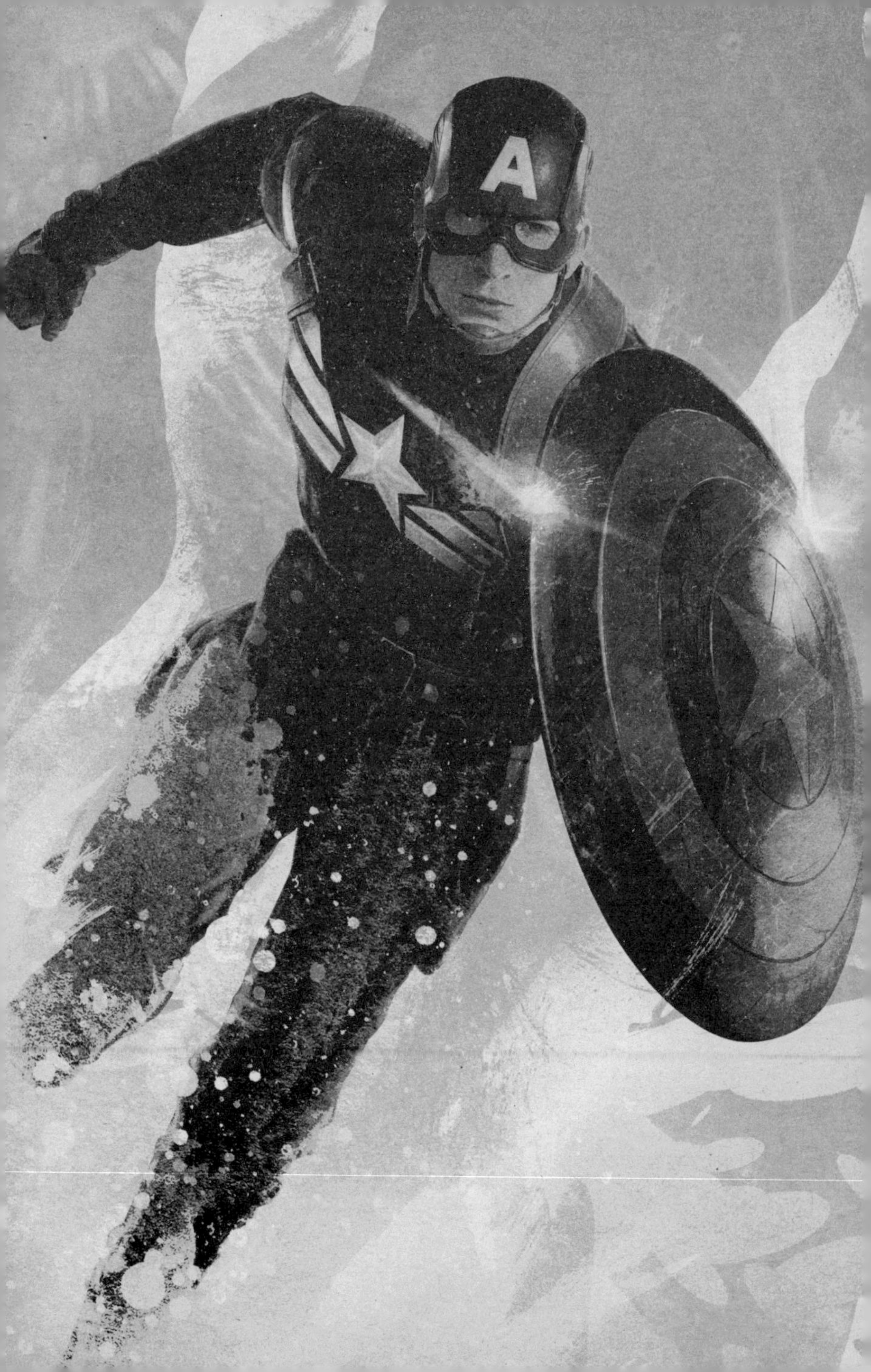

BRIEFING #13
THE CHASE

A MAN IN A HOODIE and sweatpants
made his way through the hospital. He reached the
vending machine and stopped, pulling off his hood.
Steve Rogers looked at himself in the reflection
of the glass. He had to find out who this mystery-
masked man was. Why Nick Fury was attacked. And
what was on that hard drive, which was not where he
had put it.

Then Steve noticed someone standing behind
him in the reflection of the vending machine, watching him and popping gum: Natasha Romanoff.
With lightning-fast speed, Steve whirled around
and grabbed her, pinning her arms to her side and

propelling them both through a door into the next room, where he slammed her against the wall.

"Where is it?" he hissed.

"Safe."

"Do better—"

But before Steve could finish, Natasha reversed the hold and slammed him against the wall.

"Is that better?" she asked. Then she pulled out the data device. "Where did you get this?"

"Fury gave it to me."

"Why?" Natasha asked with resentment in her tone.

"I don't know."

"Because," she sighed, "he trusted *you*."

"What's on it?" Steve asked.

"I don't know."

"That's hard to buy, since you're the one who stole it in the first place," Steve said, referring to the *Lemurian Star* hostage crisis.

"I only act like I know everything, Rogers."

"Do you know who hired the pirates?" Steve asked suspiciously.

"No. But I know who attacked Fury."

Steve's eyes grew wide.

"Most of the intelligence community doesn't believe he exists. The ones who do call him the Winter Soldier. He's credited with over two dozen assassinations in the last fifty years."

"That's not possible," Steve said referring to the time span.

"Neither are you," Natasha replied. They took a moment to let that thought sink in. Then she continued: "Five years ago, I was escorting a nuclear engineer out of Iran. Somebody shot out my tires near Odessa. We lost control and went straight off a cliff. I pulled us out but"—Natasha looked down, deep in thought—"the Winter Soldier was there. I was covering my engineer. So he shot him—right through me. Soviet slug. No rifling." She raised her shirt and showed Steve a scar that marred her abdomen.

Natasha continued. "Going after him is a dead end. I've tried. He's a ghost."

"So what do we do?"

Natasha held up the data drive. "Find out what the ghost wants."

They left the hospital, jumped in her car, and peeled off, determined to find more answers. As they talked about what might be on the data drive, they heard a loud humming coming from overhead. Natasha leaned out the driver's-side window and looked up. Her eyes grew wide with fear. It was a set of high-tech choppers, and inside the lead chopper was the Winter Soldier!

Natasha immediately went into survival mode and took evasive action with the vehicle, swerving and dodging, in case the chopper fired on them. Steve climbed halfway out of the passenger-side window and hurled his shield at the chopper. It broke the glass windshield before it ricocheted and returned to him.

The second helicopter advanced, with the Winter Soldier shouting orders. Steve saw him preparing to fire a rocket launcher at their car. He had to act fast. He grabbed Natasha and they jumped out of the speeding vehicle, just in the nick of time! The pilot pressed a button and a set of missiles collided with their vehicle! A huge explosion rang out and destroyed the car as Steve and Natasha skidded down the pavement to a safe stop aboard Cap's shield.

Using the flames as cover, Steve and Natasha quickly escaped into the nearby woods as the helicopters landed. The Winter Soldier and his mercenaries hopped out and looked through the rubble, trying to find them. But they came up empty-handed, again. The Winter Soldier was angry. He slammed his metal arm into the wrecked vehicle and it skidded down the street. The S.H.I.E.L.D. agents had escaped with the data drive.

Steve and Natasha were safe for now, but they needed help and Steve knew just who to ask.

THE EXO-7 FILE

HOME FROM A RUN on the National
Mall, a sweaty Sam reached for the orange juice in his
fridge and gulped it down, quenching his thirst. Suddenly, there was a knock at the door, and he headed
to answer it. Must be Girl Scouts or something, he
thought. When he answered the door, though, it
wasn't Girl Scouts. Not in the least bit.

There stood Steve and Natasha, out of breath,
faces dirty, clothes torn.

"Hey, man," Sam said, taken aback.

"Sorry about this," Steve said, trying to find the
words to explain, "but we need a place to lie low."

Sam stared for a minute, still in shock. It's not

every day that Captain America and Black Widow come to you asking for help. Finally, he opened his door and invited them in.

Later, a freshly showered Steve exited the bathroom to find Natasha sitting on the couch, lost in thought. He cracked a smile to ease her thoughts and Natasha raised an eyebrow. They had been through a lot, but at least they had each other's backs and they were grateful to be partners.

"There's breakfast, if you guys eat that sort of thing!" yelled Sam from the kitchen. The aroma of bacon and eggs filled the apartment. Sam grabbed toast from the toaster and placed it on a plate.

"Fake butter or real?" Sam asked Steve.

"Dry," Steve retorted with a smirk.

Natasha and Steve ate breakfast over the data drive, which lay in the center of the kitchen table. Steve trusted Sam, especially since he was a fellow soldier. They had a bond and Steve felt comfortable filling Sam in on what had happened with Fury and the Winter Soldier. He told Sam they couldn't defeat this menace and his army alone and they were running out of answers and places to turn. They asked Sam to hide the data drive in a safe spot, since no one but them would know it was there. Sam felt honored and obliged.

He watched the two broken S.H.I.E.L.D. agents eat quietly. Then it hit him. He left the kitchen and went upstairs, where he rummaged through a box of files. Natasha and Steve just looked at each other as they heard boxes moving above. Finally, Sam raced back and tossed a file onto the table right between them.

"What is this?" Steve asked.

"Call it a résumé," Sam said with a smile.

Natasha picked up a photo of Sam and another soldier. Behind them were white-capped mountains.

Natasha studied the photo. "Is that Bakmala? Khalid Khadil mission? Was that you?" She looked to Steve. "You didn't say he was a pararescue."

Steve reviewed the picture. "Is that Riley?"

Stoic, Sam nodded.

"I heard they couldn't bring in choppers because of the rocket-propelled grenades," Natasha said to Sam. "What did you use? Stealth suits?"

"No," Sam said, tapping on a file that read EXO-7 FALCON. "These."

Steve was confused. "I thought you were a pilot."

"I never said 'pilot,'" Sam replied.

Steve shook his head. This was dangerous stuff. But he knew Sam was up for the task. A soldier always is.

Natasha and Steve glanced at each other. For a moment, maybe, just maybe . . . this could work.

"Where could we get ourselves one of these?" Steve asked Sam.

"Officially, the only ones left are at Fort Meade, behind three guarded gates and twelve inches of steel door." And then Sam smiled. "But there is one more." He looked out the window to a shed in his backyard. Steve and Natasha followed his gaze. They were in business.

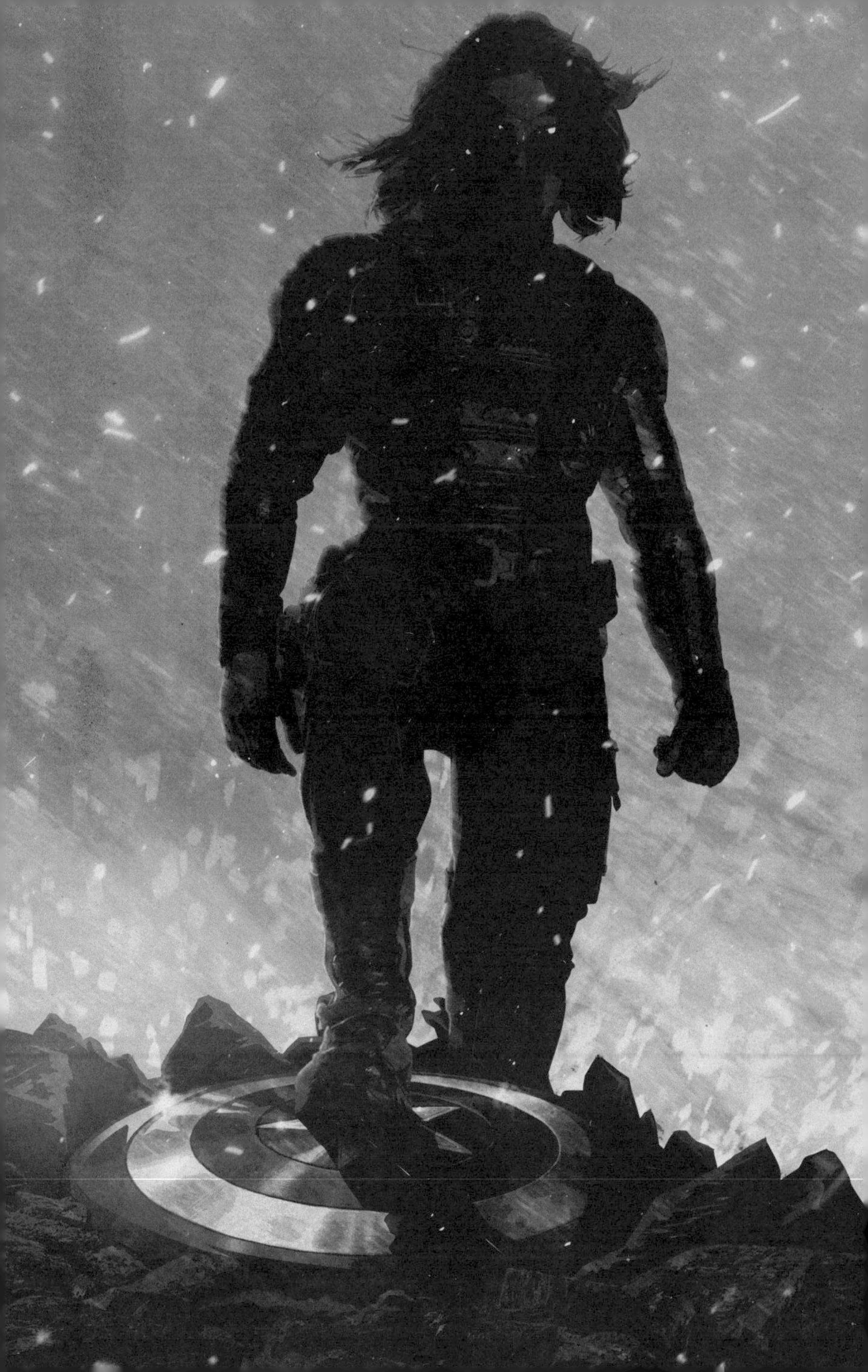

BRIEFING #15

FALCON TAKES FLIGHT

REPORTS OF A MAN flying high above the streets came in from throughout the city of Washington, D.C. It wasn't far-fetched to the citizens, especially after the battle in New York City with the Avengers. Perhaps it was Thor or Iron Man, they thought. But this man was different. This man had wings.

Steve and Natasha, now in their Captain America and Black Widow costumes, parkoured from roof to roof in downtown D.C. with ease. As fast as they were going, they were still working to keep up with their new friend.

Donning his Exo-7 Falcon wings, Sam Wilson, now known as Falcon to Cap and Black Widow, flew high above them. Occasionally, Falcon rose over the buildings of downtown Washington to get a bird's-eye view of his entire city. He was keeping an eye out for any trace of the Winter Soldier and his mercenaries as Cap and Black Widow trailed behind. All seemed quiet, but that was about to change.

Falcon pointed into the distance: a bunch of high-tech choppers—armed to the teeth with missiles and rocket launchers—was flying in their direction. As the choppers got closer, they saw that one of the men hanging over the side was the Winter Soldier!

Noticing that the helicopter's guns were aimed directly at Falcon, Cap gripped his shield and ran faster than he had ever run before, right toward the choppers. He leaped over pipes and roofs and slid under railings with the grace of a jaguar. Cap jumped and held his vibranium shield against his shoulder, blocking the incoming fire.

Now realizing it would take something more powerful to destroy Cap's shield, the helicopter's pilot

started to fly away to regroup with the other choppers. Cap yelled to Falcon to give him a boost. They
couldn't let it get away.

Falcon swooped down, grabbed Captain America,
and was flying him up when the choppers circled back!
One flew straight for Black Widow. Another hovered
as the Winter Soldier hung out the passenger-side
door, urging Cap and Falcon on. He wanted a fight!

"I'll take him!" Cap shouted. "You get the other
one!"

Falcon tossed Captain America into the open door
of the helicopter, right behind the Winter Soldier,
then flew away to stop the one that was in pursuit of
Black Widow.

As Falcon made his way toward Black Widow
another chopper fired down on him. Falcon dipped
and dived and dodged the incoming fire with ease,
eventually losing his assailant. He smirked as he sliced
through the air in his Exo-7 suit. He hadn't lost his
touch.

PARAM3 3T_8900_15TGFFK-3 THKK-90
3K_HJ041556-9-5P0043899-160-R8LZ
TEAS-32-89-JKIDD_09021-JK05-4-465

THE SUPER-SOLDIER VERSUS THE WINTER SOLDIER

THE SUPER-SOLDIER and the Winter Soldier faced off inside the back of the chopper until the masked man gave a mighty metal punch to Cap, knocking him out of the helicopter toward the busy streets below! Cap fell and crashed through the roof of a city bus!

Captain America stumbled between the seats, trying to regain his composure. But he couldn't do so because the driver swerved and barreled violently through an intersection, crashing into a parked car and sending Cap flying down the aisle.

Determined, the Winter Soldier jumped down

after Captain America, but just as he was about to attack, Black Widow appeared to help her comrade. She fired her sidearm at the Winter Soldier, but he blocked the ammunition with his metal arm and it *tinged* off in every direction. Then he raised his rocket launcher. Black Widow's eyes grew wide as she leaped behind a sedan to avoid the explosive fire.

KABOOM! She agilely dodged another blast and then fired a grappling hook into a freeway overpass, allowing her to swing neatly to the street below.

The other helicopters landed and dozens of mercenaries piled out. The Winter Soldier gave them orders to go after the fallen Super-Soldier, who was still stuck in the bus, while he continued to go after Black Widow.

Back in the bus, Steve sat up, woozy. He had taken quite a fall, but he wasn't badly injured. He looked around for his shield, but it was wasn't in the bus. Must have lost it during the fall, he thought. Just then, he heard the *CLANK CLANK CLANK* of a Gatling gun powering up!

Cap saw the bus driver trying to exit the bus. "Get

down, now!" he yelled. The driver threw himself to the floor and Captain America got to his feet, racing to the front of the bus as the massive Gatling gun fired from outside, decimating the back end of the bus.

Cap dove out of the bus and landed just inches from his shield. He was reaching for it when he looked up and saw a merc waiting for him. The merc raised his weapon to Captain America, but before he could fire, there was a loud *WHOOSH!*

It was Falcon! He swooped in and knocked the merc out, saving Cap! Falcon and Steve shared a look and Falcon flew back into the sky to battle more of the Winter Soldier's goons. Cap smiled. I guess having Falcon join us was a good idea, he thought. But his moment was interrupted by another *CLANK CLANK CLANK*. He turned just in time. Bullets met his shield with great force, pushing Cap back. The First Avenger gave his shield his shoulder and leaned into the blasts from the Gatling gun.

Down the street, the Winter Soldier clenched his fists with rage and walked toward the intersection. All was quiet except for a few abandoned cars that still had their engines running. A siren wailed and a cop car came around a corner and screeched to a halt. Two officers jumped out and raised their weapons, but without hesitation, the Winter Soldier raised his rocket launcher and fired at the car, sending the cops fleeing for cover and the vehicle into the air in a burst of flames. Pedestrians ran for safety as the Winter Soldier approached a truck and rolled a silver ball underneath it. Suddenly, Black Widow fled from behind the truck and dove behind another vehicle. Within seconds the truck blew high into the sky, debris falling everywhere as a war zone unfolded in the streets.

Winter Soldier checked behind the vehicle that Black Widow had dived behind, but she wasn't there. As the masked man scanned the area for her, Black Widow silently crept up and leaped toward him.

"This doesn't end like Odessa. . . ." she said, firing her Widow's Bites! Like magnets, they stuck to his metal arm, shocking him and momentarily causing the arm to go limp. Puzzled and enraged, the

Winter Soldier studied his useless limb as Black Widow scrambled away.

Back by the bus, Captain America leaned into the gunfire as the Gatling gun fired on him, pushing him back. He fought on and pushed his way closer and closer to the merc. More mercs came to help refill the Gatling, but Falcon swooped in and carried them off! Finally, the Gatling gun ran dry. *Click. Click. Click.* The merc behind it gaped as Cap hammered him down.

Citizens popped their heads out from behind buildings and cars, curious if the coast was clear. Black Widow ran through the intersection as she fled the Winter Soldier.

"Get to safety!" she cried to the pedestrians. With all the chaos unfolding around her, Black Widow's main priority was keeping the people of D.C. safe from harm. As she fled past a sedan, a metal ball flew through the air and landed on the hood of the car. Before she could react, the windshield exploded, sending her diving to the pavement, wincing in pain. She looked behind her and saw, twenty yards away, the Winter Soldier advancing relentlessly. As she raised her Widow's Bite to fire, the Winter Soldier drew his weapon and fired first. Black Widow dodged out of the way and was pinned down behind the car with nowhere to go.

The Winter Soldier climbed atop the sedan and looked down at the injured Black Widow, who looked up, unable to protect herself anymore. This could be the end. . . .

Suddenly, Captain America, shield raised, launched through the air right at the Winter Soldier! With a battle cry he prepared to strike the Winter Soldier, but instead, the villain turned with his metal fist and it CLANGED against Cap's vibranium shield, sending a shock wave in every direction.

They both flew back a few feet, in awe at the power of the impact. The Winter Soldier quickly raised his weapon and emptied a clip into Cap's shield. Then he leaped over a car toward Cap and yanked his shield from his hands. The Winter Soldier drew another weapon, but Cap blocked his hand and the weapon slid under a nearby car. They exchanged a flurry of punches, each harder than the one before. The Winter Soldier backed up and pulled out a knife, ready to attack. Cap knuckled up and waved to the Winter Soldier to bring it. Steve dodged slash after slash, finally kicking the knife away.

More sirens wailed in the distance and scores of SWAT and army vehicles closed in on the scene and began to surround the massive battle between the Super-Soldier and the Winter Soldier. Helicopters hovered overhead and watched. An audience was born as dozens of pedestrians came out of hiding to observe the intense fight.

Captain America punched and the Winter Soldier kicked. They began to grow tired but they kept on, never letting up. Not even an inch. Then the Winter Soldier pulled out a series of small metal spheres and tossed them at Cap, who quickly dove, grabbing his shield. A blast impacted the scratched and bruised shield, but it held up, protecting Captain America just as it had time and time again. But the blast also blew Cap back across the intersection and into a van, crushing its side.

The Winter Soldier advanced on Cap, who got to his feet just as the masked man threw a punch. Cap grabbed him and flipped him over his head. As he did so, his hand grabbed part of the Winter Soldier's mask, so when the villain landed on the concrete, something was missing. His mask. It was in Captain America's hand.

"Bucky?" Steve said in awe as he stared into the eyes of his long-lost friend. But something was wrong. It had been seventy years since he'd seen his child-hood buddy. But he hadn't physically changed one bit.

"Who the heck is Bucky?" the Winter Soldier asked, looking back at Cap with a blank stare.

Steve lowered his shield, unsure what to make of this.

That gave the Winter Soldier his chance. He looked up as one of the helicopters lowered right over them. He leaped onto the hood of a car, jumped high into the sky, and grabbed the chopper's landing skid as it took off.

Steve couldn't move. Black Widow was injured. Falcon was helping civilians out from under the debris.

The police were trying to restore order. Everything was chaos. But Captain America knew one thing: he would see Bucky again. And the next time they met, Steve would get answers. . . .

CLOSING STATEMENT

To: S.H.I.E.L.D. Agent ████████████

From: Agent Sitwell

The World Security Council would like to have a full report regarding the above briefings. Alexander Pierce will be attending, so make sure your report is top notch. And, if history repeats itself, Fury will be combing every single inch of your files, so, take it from me, make it perfect. The World Security Council will be looking for answers. It is up to you to provide them with answers. Please provide your report to Maria Hill once executed. Until then, S.H.I.E.L.D.

will continue to collect data. We have a feeling this Winter Soldier character and his team of mercs are far from done. Good thing we have a Super-Soldier on our side. . . .

Best,

Agent Sitwell

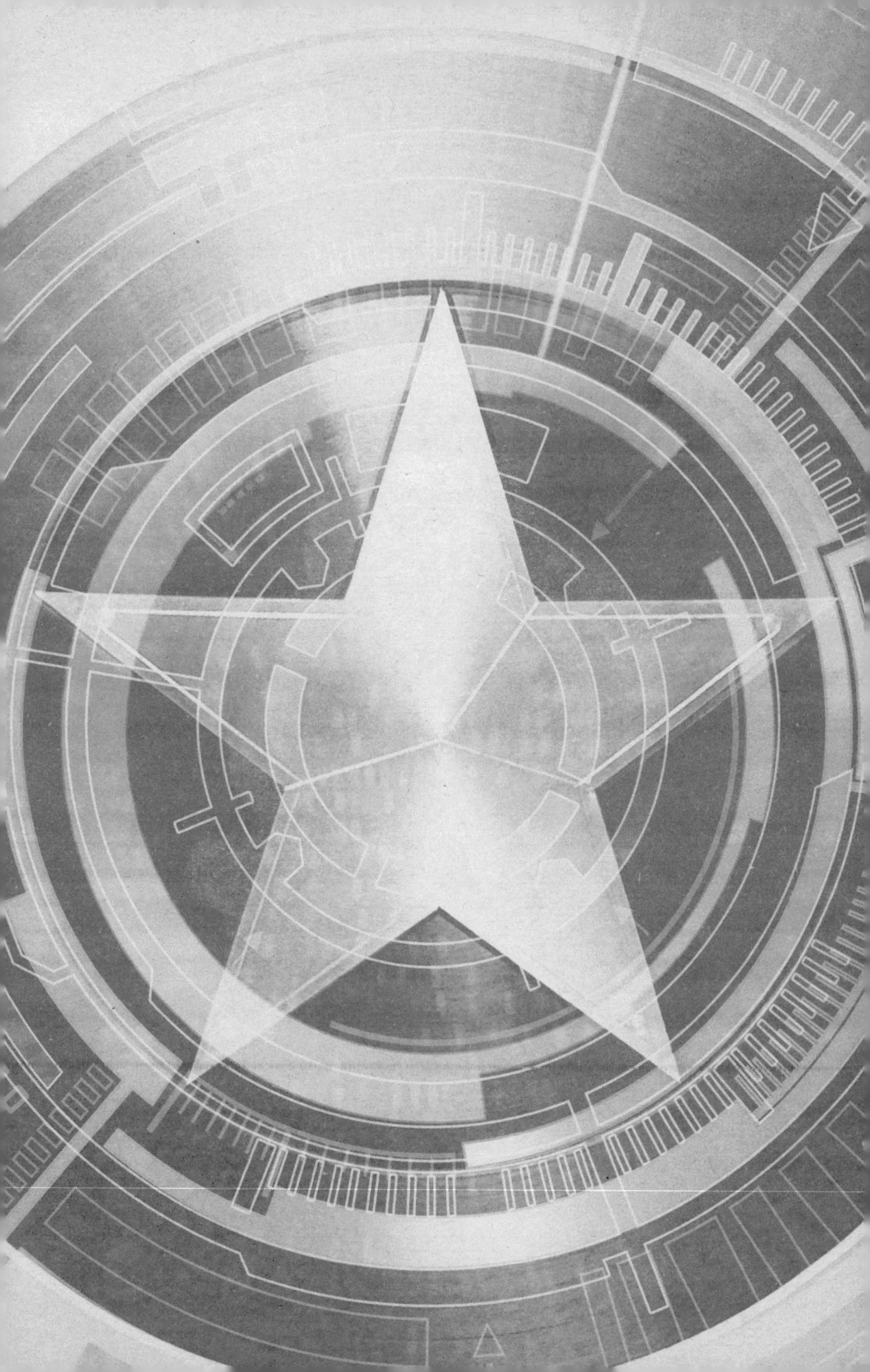

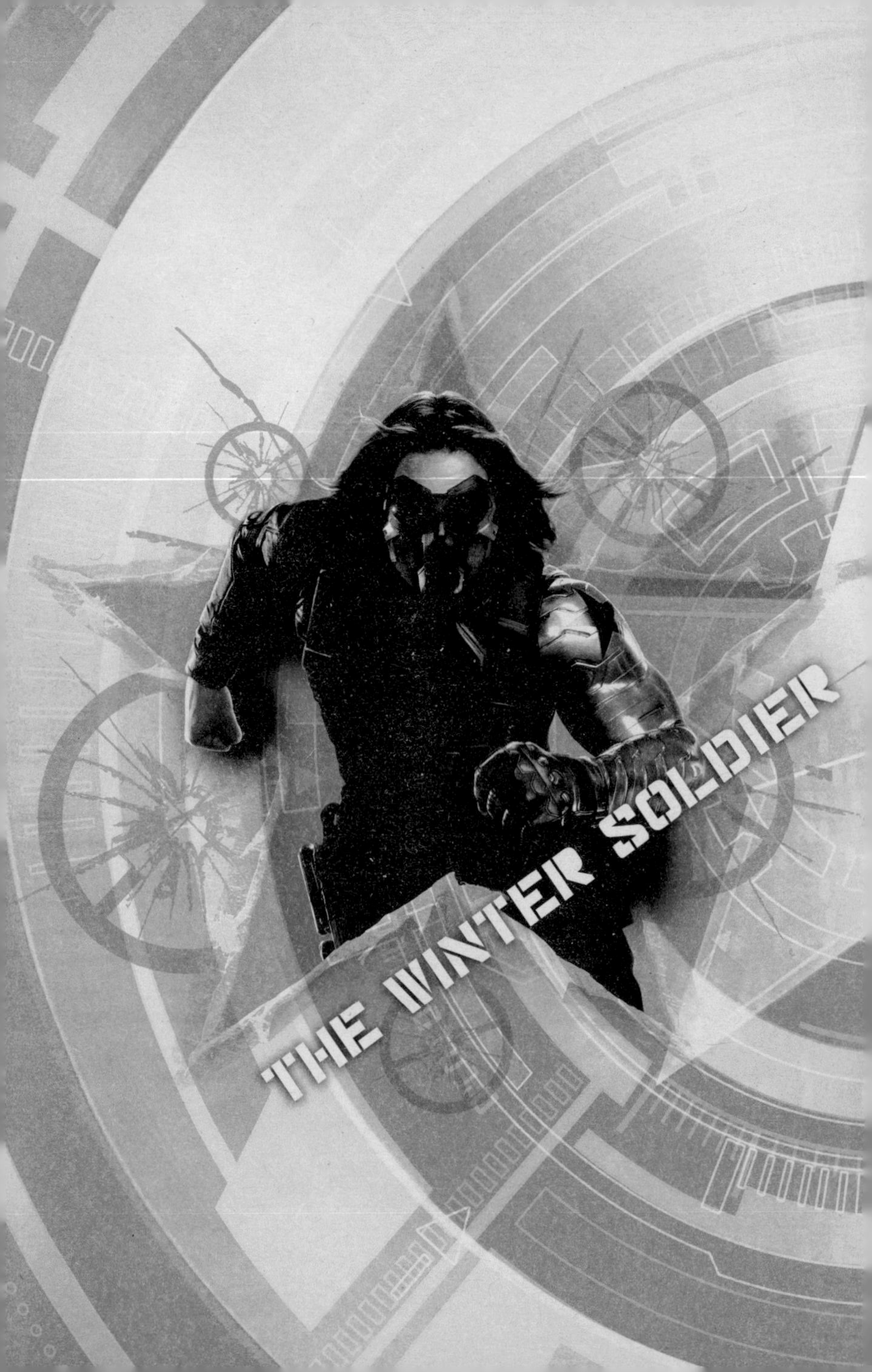
THE WINTER SOLDIER

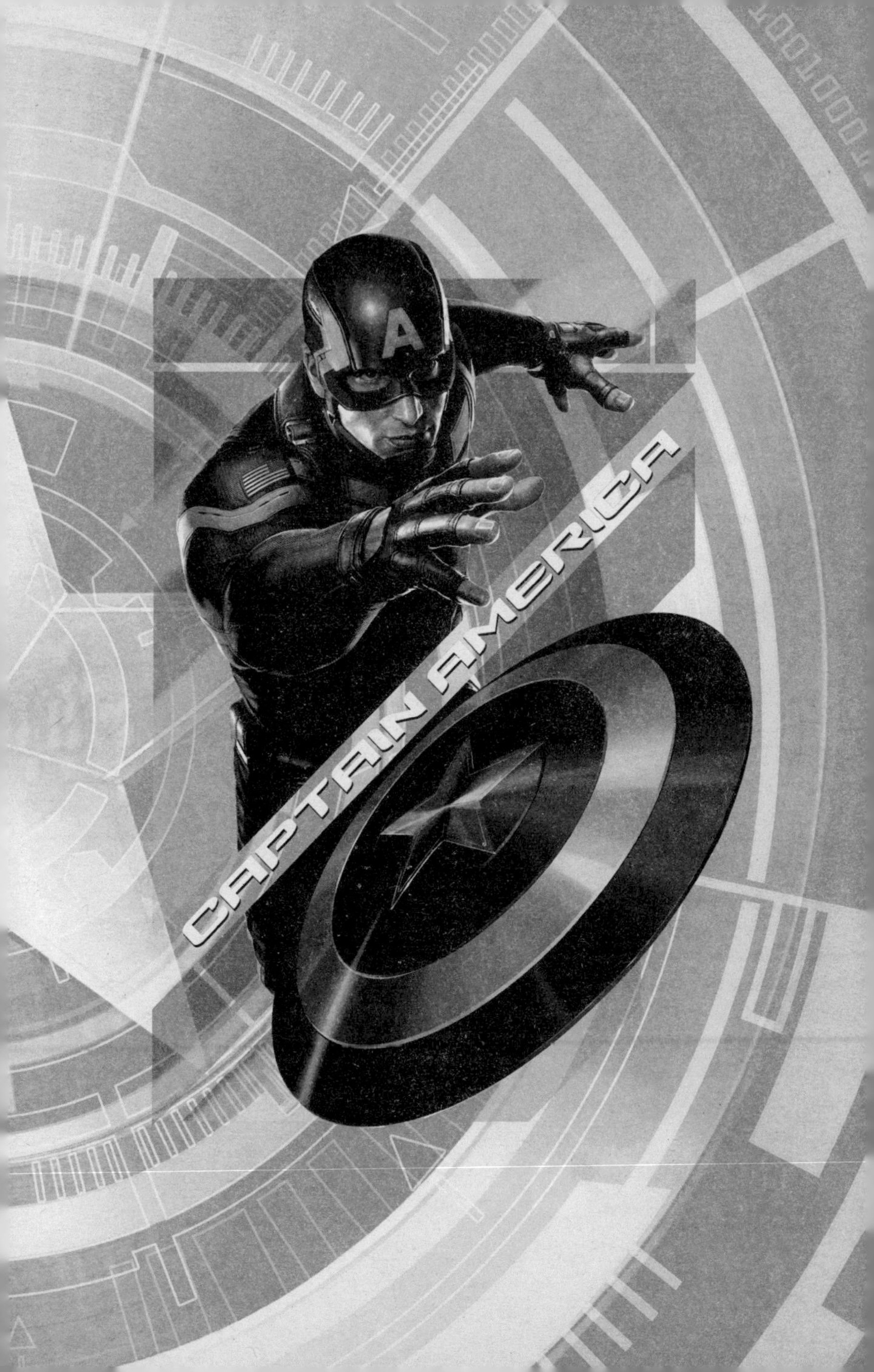
CAPTAIN AMERICA

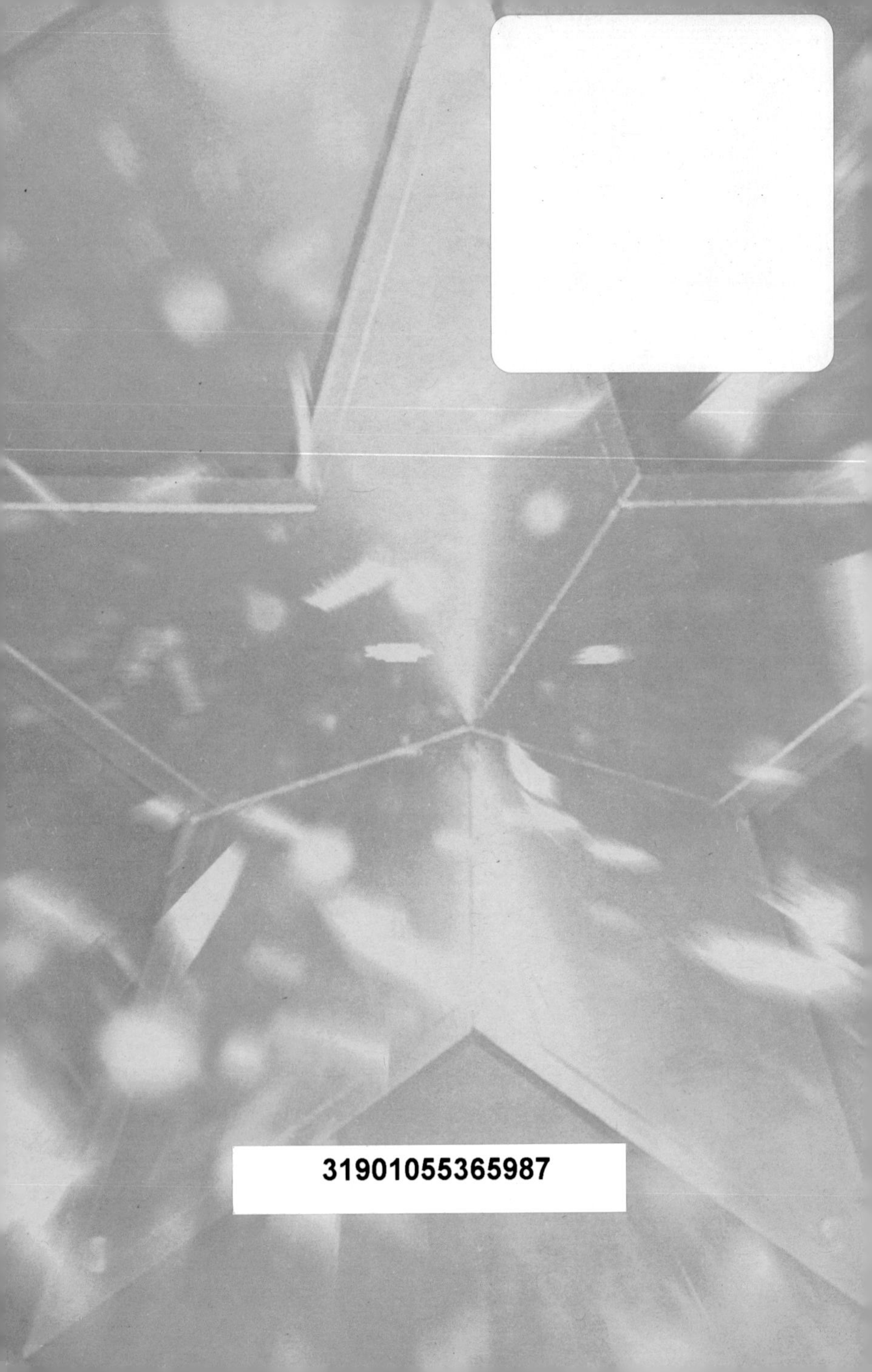